Katschen

The Book of Joseph

Katschen

TRANSLATED BY DAVID KRISS

&

The Book of Joseph

TRANSLATED BY ALAN TREISTER
WITH EDDY LEVENSTON

YOEL HOFFMANN

A New Directions Book

Katschen & The Book of Joseph is published by arrangement with The Harris/Elon Agency and the Keter Publishing Company of Jerusalem, Israel.

Note: The Publisher gratefully thanks Rosmarie Waldrop for bringing the work of Yoel Hoffmann to New Directions' attention.

Design by Semadar Megged
First published clothbound in 1998
Manufactured in the United States of America
New Directions Books are printed on acid-free paper.
Published simultaneously in Canada by Penguin Books Canad; Limited

Library of Congress Cataloging-in-Publication Data:
Hoffmann, Yoel.
[Katskhen. English]
Katschen ; & The Book of Joseph / Yoel Hoffmann.
p. cm.
Contains Katskhen translated by David Kriss and Sefer Yosef translated by Alan Treister with Eddy Levenston.
ISBN 0-8112-1373-0 (alk. paper)
I. Kriss, David. II. Treister, Alan. III. Levenston, Edward A.
IV. Hoffmann, Yoel. Sefer Yosef. English. V. Title. VI. Title:
Book of Joseph.
PJ5054.H6319K3813 1998
892.4'36—dc21   97-50300
                                                                  CIP

New Directions Books are published for James Laughlin
by New Directions Publishing Corporation,
80 Eighth Avenue, New York 10011

Contents

The Book of
Joseph

F O R E W O R D[1]

And when Professor Dov Beharot (formerly called Berl Zunshprenklekh) received this manuscript, he read in it what he read and said:

My advice
To the author is
That he send his work
To Leib Gutharz
The author of
The well-known book
"Strength out of the Abyss." And if
His work pleases
My friend Leib
(Who has in the meantime
Changed his
Name to Lavi Lev-Tov)
He will see
To it that
The author is
Enrolled in
The Writers' Union
And that the book
Is published.

And Leib Gutharz too read in it what he read and his wrath was kindled and he thought to himself, "Oh, the solar

<hr>

[1] Printed on the back cover of the Hebrew edition.

eclipse" or "A dog-faced generation." And he also thought "Why on earth did my friend Berl forward such a composition to my address?"

It did once indeed occur to this author that he could write a book that is all blank pages. There is no doubt that such a book is far superior to any other. But while he was entertaining this idea in his mind, a certain American, more industrious than himself, offered such a manuscript to a certain publisher. And the publisher, who was also American, invested what he invested and printed the book and millions of Americans bought it and read it and their hearts rejoiced. And that American is now as rich as Croesus and need not add a single word to his writings until the day he dies.

But this book about Joseph Silverman was sewn by Joseph Silverman himself, and the author found it intact, like the suits sewn by Joseph. Only here and there remained a few unwoven threads. And like Joseph's needle, Gurnisht's organ also went in and out. Thus it is fit to be made a prayer book for the devout.

And what is the significance of all these events? Many movements are better than a single movement, whether up or down. Many movements from right to left (or from left to right) should be preferred to many movements up and down. But if one can not multiply one's movements to right and left, one should move up and down, rather than resort to a single movement.

THE BOOK OF JOSEPH

"HERR ZILBERMANN, THESE DAYS EVERYONE sews on a Singer," the Singer agent said and removed his hat. Several streets away, on the Friedrichstrasse, Siegfried Stopf stared at his legs. A golden down already covered his thighs. He moved the muscle above his knee and the muscle moved. "Na," Siegfried thought. One could leave the story right there, at that very moment, in the Berlin of nineteen hundred and thirty-two. The agent would put on his hat again, and would say what he would say and would take it off again and put it on the tailor's table once again, and then remove his hat for the third time and say what he said, and so on and so forth. And Siegried Stopf would stare at his legs and not take his eyes off them as long as the Singer agent was putting his hat on and taking it off. Had things remained thus, Joseph Silverman would be sewing the trousers of Herr Wehrmus, the law clerk, to this day. But Joseph Silverman finished Herr Wehrmus's trousers that very week and the hair on Siegfried Stopf's legs grew dark and things ran on until in nineteen hundred and thirty-eight what happened happened.

The Singer agent sat down at the tailor's bench and placed a foot on the treadle. The metal wheel revolved and the needle inside the machine vibrated like the devil. Joseph Silverman remembered how after Sabbath afternoon prayers, Reb Zeylig would pick up his violin. His right hand would hold the bow and whirl like the wind, and the fingers of his left

hand would rise and fall until one's soul hovered in the upper worlds.

"Herr Zilbermann, you don't have to pay it all at once. One
payment, now, and the rest in the middle of each month."
Yingele saw in his mind's eye the picture of his father whom
the German had politely multiplied into many people, ap-
pearing one after another in the middle of every month, as
the moon becomes full, holding a banknote in their outstretched hands.

When the German left and took the Singer sewing-machine
with him, Joseph Silverman picked up the needle, held it between forefinger and thumb, spread out his other three fingers like a wing, and with a movement first slow and then
faster and faster, drove it in and out of Herr Wehrmus's
trousers. Then he turned the trousers over, held the tip of
the needle in the fingers of his other hand and pulled the
thread ever upward.

When the agent took the sewing machine and went on his
way, Gurnisht understood that Joseph disliked the machine
with its needle that rose and fell as though possessed. But the
revolving silver wheel had pleased Gurnisht. Once Gurnisht
had looked at a machine called a Gramophone and thought
about the grooves on the disc. These grooves, he thought to
himself, turn into sounds in the air that people call music.
Why shouldn't these sounds turn into light as well? There is
this groove that sounds a "La" and another that sounds a
"Do." So, why don't those so-called engineers take the trouble to rummage through their teachings and add wires and
lamps to the gramophone that would turn the grooves into
light? They could, for example, turn the groove whose sound

is "La" into a patch of green light and the groove whose sound is "Do" into a patch of red light; or they could turn the groove of a languid sound into pale moonlight and the groove of a fierce sound into dazzling sunlight. The listeners would then see the sounds, just like on Mt. Sinai. And the engineers would be compensated for their labor and he, Gurnisht, would gain great wealth from his invention, after he had duly recorded it in the office called the "Büro für Erfindungen." But, when Gurnisht related this matter to Joseph, Joseph said that the sounds heard on Mt. Sinai came from heaven and this is nothing like the machine with which the gentile makes music.

Siegfried Stopf put his foot down on the floor. Then he put on leather pants called "knickerbockers." "Na," he thought to himself, "Now I look good enough to ride a bicycle."

The memory of Reb Zeylig and his violin reminded Joseph of his father, Reb Chaim, who would put a bucket of water beside his bed and in the morning when he opened his eyes would dip his hands in, still lying down, in order not to move, God forbid, even the shortest distance without washing his hands. In other matters, however, Reb Chaim was not so strict. Once, Joseph (whose name then was Yosl, not Josef in the German style) went into the apple orchard of a widow, and for his trouble the widow thrashed him with a stick. When his mother saw the bruises on his back, she grabbed his hand, pulled him to the widow's house, set herself in the doorway and said, "You just wait until my husband comes home." Meanwhile all the Jews of the town gathered around to wait and see what Reb Chaim would do to the widow. And when Reb Chaim returned from the

synagogue they all surrounded him and told him, all together and in many voices, what had happened. When the
widow saw Reb Chaim, her face turned as white as lime.
And when Reb Chaim saw her white face, he went into her
house, took a glass of water and brought it to her lips. The
widow sipped some water with her teeth chattering against
the glass, and Yosl's mother looked at Reb Chaim, her husband, in amazement. At this the onlookers' curiosity abated,
and they all went home. And when Yosl also came home his
mother said, "Your father's a good man, but his head is in the
clouds." A few years later when Reb Chaim's eyes weakened
he went to the shop that sold glasses. The shopkeeper put
glasses on his nose and told him to read a book and see the
size of the letters. Among the books lying there Reb Chaim
found a Hasidic book and sat down to read it. The shopkeeper, who was busy with other customers, paid no more
attention to Reb Chaim and Reb Chaim, for whom the letters had now moved closer, sat and read in the book until
dark and it was time to shut up shop.

Afterwards, Yosl's mother stepped on a rotten board, fell
into the cellar, and died. When Reb Chaim had buried his
wife and returned home, he burst into tears and said over
and over again, "Completely torn from its roots." When he
calmed down, Yosl asked if she had risen to heaven and Reb
Chaim said that she had been a righteous woman, and therefore the deeper the fall, the higher the ascent. And, when
Yosl was Bar Mitzvahed, they both went to the synagogue
and Reb Chaim said a blessing, thanking God that he was
no longer responsible, but at the same time reached out his
hand and touched Yosl's hair, and Yosl was not afraid his father would leave him.

When Yosl came of age, his father told him that "forty days before birth, Heaven declares the partners to the betrothal," and this was why he would have to be married off to Chaya-Leah. Then he told him that when Yosl's mother was still in the cradle, the former Rabbi felt her skull and declared that in' days to come this baby would be married off to Reb Chaim, who was also a baby at the time.

And when Yosl's father died, the Rabbi said, "Reb Chaim was an observant Jew," and his body was wrapped in the shroud. And when Yosl was saying Kaddish, the shroud moved and Yosl imagined his father inside the shroud folding his arms and twiddling his hands and circling his thumbs as he did after Sabbath dinner when he felt at his best.

Afterwards Joseph brought home knitted stockings that were faulty, took up his needle, and repaired the faults. And the owner of the stockings sold his stockings to Russians who covered their feet with them on wintry days. In the evenings, Chaya-Leah also took up a needle and sat next to Joseph. Once she asked Joseph if he was sorry that she had been married off to him, and her face turned red.

That same year, in Berlin, Hans Stopf mounted his wife. First he pushed her onto the bed and pulled up her dress. Then he took off his trousers and stuck the member that was between his legs into her body. Then he said, "Na! Jetzt geh'n wir mal schlafen."[1] But that very same movement had joggled Siegfried and moved him out of Hans's body into the egg in Lotte. At first, Siegfried was no more than a black

1. German - "That's it. Now let's go to sleep."

stain on the egg, but as time passed the stain swelled and took on the shape of a tadpole. And hands and feet extended from that tadpole.

When a frog jumped into the water of the ritual bath where the Jews purified their bodies, they asked the Rabbi "Has the water been defiled?" The Rabbi studied the holy books and declared, "Animals do not defile, only man." Joseph knew, with some kind of wondrous knowledge, that the Jews who stood there saw only the frog's leap, but the Rabbi saw with a different kind of vision how the frog sank in the water, then came up and slowly floated on the surface, still powered by the same jump, its feet spread out behind it. For seven years Joseph inserted his body between Chaya-Leah's loins and finally, from that same movement, his seed was planted in her womb. The seed floated and rose in Chaya-Leah's fluids and slowly became Yingele. And in nineteen hundred and twenty-eight, when the Cossacks killed Chaya-Leah with an axe, Joseph picked up the infant, walked twelve leagues to the train station, and fled from Russia. On that day the image of the frog came back to his memory, but the frog did not return to the surface of the water. It sank to the bottom of the pool like a stone.

A single movement may totally transform the course of events. In the days when Joseph Silverman was sewing the trousers of Herr Wehrmus, the law clerk, and Siegfried Stopf was looking at his legs, a philosopher called Ludwig was thinking his thoughts. First he thought in Austria, then he thought in England, and this is why he wrote a book in which he declared that human language represents a kind of picture of the world, and everything said in language reflects its form. For example, when a person says "rooster on the roof" it means that there is in the world a roof and a rooster. And between the roof and the rooster there is a certain relation called "on," and this is also found in the world, although not in exactly the same way as the rooster and roof are found. And all the other philosophers read his book and said, "Yes, that is certainly the way it is." One day that same Ludwig was sitting in a place called Cambridge having dinner with an Italian. Suddenly the Italian made a kind of movement with his hand, as is the wont of those from Naples, and Ludwig, who did not know what wordly form that movement represented, was struck dumb. His hand, which held a teaspoon, froze in its place and consequently he tasted none of the pudding. He subsequently sank into deep contemplation, and only extricated himself from it by arriving at the general theory that human language is not a picture of the world, and what is said does not represent the forms of the world. He also wrote this idea in a book etc., etc. And all because of a movement made absentmindedly by an Italian.

> And what did
> the Cossack
> think
> as he raised his axe
> on Chaya-Leah's head?
> What did he think?
> He thought
> Now
> Now

Joseph was not at all sorry that at the end of his journey he arrived in Berlin and not in America, for everything that happens is God's will. He was only sorry the trains continued running on the Sabbath. When he arrived in Berlin, autumn was well under way, and the cold pierced his bones. He wrapped the infant in his coat and asked a man where the Jews lived. And when the man asked him if he wished to go to the German Jews or the other Jews, Joseph answered, "the others," and reached a place in the north of Berlin called Alexanderplatz. And the day Joseph came to Alexanderplatz he made a vow that for the rest of his days he would imagine that Chaya-Leah had come there with him. And, in order not to forget his vow, he resolved not to call the infant by his name but "Yingele,"[1] the way Chaya-Leah did.

At that time, when Siegfried Stopf was ten years old, his aunt Gertrud and her daughter moved in. And when everyone thought that Siegfried had gone to sleep, Siegfried pricked up his ears and listened to Gertrud, who was saying in the kitchen how her husband had called her "a donkey's ass," and said that the girl was not his, and driven her out of the house. And when Gertrud washed her girl in the bathroom and Siegfried needed to urinate there, Gertrud said, "Come in, but I'll see your thing," and Siegfried went in and urinated and Gertrud put him in the bath with the girl and washed him between his legs until his thing stood up. That same year Siegfried began to play the trumpet.

The joy that Joseph had known when Chaya-Leah was alive came back only once, when he suffered from a stomachache and went to a doctor. That doctor was a gentile who loved the sight of bearded Jews who spoke the Jewish language. After he explained to Joseph the difference between the "Alte Testament" and "Neue Testament," he instructed him to bathe in a sulphur spring that was not in Berlin, but in a

---

1. Yiddish - "Dear child."

German village in the mountains. And when Joseph said, "I'll go when I can," the doctor said, "Immediately," and picked up the telephone and asked to speak with Herr Doktor Schmidt of the health clinic at the spa. When he heard Herr Doktor Schmidt's voice over the receiver, the doctor in Berlin asked after the health of his "dear Vife" and several others. When this part of the conversation was over, the Berliner asked Herr Doktor Schmidt if he would be so kind as to take in an "armer Schneider"[1] whose liver had betrayed him. He also said that Herr Doktor Schmidt would find the Jew interesting since the Jewish language was nothing but archaic German. Then he ordered Joseph to come the next day. And when Joseph came with Yingele, the doctor was not flustered at all, and accompanied father and son to the railway station, where he bought them bread and sausage. And although the doctor understood something of the Jewish language and knew that the Jews study Talmud, he was not versed in the dietary laws.

When they arrived in the village and found Herr Doktor Schmidt, he settled them in a small room with only one bed in it. But the next day when Joseph opened his eyes and looked out of the window, he saw forests and snow on the summit of the mountain. He took Yingele's hand and went outside to walk along the paths of the village which had no more than a dozen wooden houses. When they had gone some distance from the village, the path gradually shrank in size and birds rose up in the forest. And when Joseph and Yingele climbed up the slopes of the mountain and came out of the forest, there was a patch of white cloud above them. First, Joseph's head and then their four feet disappeared into

---

1. German - "poor tailor."

the cloud. The cloud hid the world from sight and covered Joseph's body and Yingele's body with a kind of extremely thin vapor. At that moment Joseph felt again a happiness in his chest that he had known once before. When they descended from the cloud Yingele's hand was wet.

Hallelujah
A cloud descends from Heaven.
From the abyss rises Joseph Silverman
Now his beard is in the cloud:
Whiteness touches
White.

For several days Siegfried Stopf had noticed that Brunhilde Weber was making eyes at him. "She is a piece of ass worthy of the name," he thought, "but I'll have to ask Karl if she puts out."

When they returned to the clinic Herr Doktor Schmidt asked Joseph if he had found the mountain scenery pleasing and Joseph said he had. And Herr Doktor Schmidt asked Joseph from where he had come to Germany, and Joseph said he came from Russia, and Herr Doktor Schmidt said the scenery in Russia was also beautiful though its beauty was somewhat crude. Then Herr Doktor Schmidt asked Joseph if he knew the folk etymology connected with the name of the village and Joseph said he did not. And Herr Doktor Schmidt said that the village was called "Kannitverstehen," and recounted how it was first settled by a tribe that suffered from deafness. After they had built their wooden houses, they sat down in their doorways and looked at the path that climbed up from the valley to see who might visit their village. But when the people of the valley came up to the village and greeted its inhabitants, these could only answer "Kann nit verstehen" which in German means "I do not understand." And that is why the people of the valley assumed that the name of the village was Kannitverstehen and called it by that name. When Yingele asked if the people around there were deaf, Herr Doktor Schmidt laughed and said that there were no deaf people there except one, whose mother had boxed his ears.

Because Siegfried Stopf's skin had broken out in pimples, he did not like the look of his face in the mirror. But when he looked in the glass of the store window on Friedrichstrasse he couldn't see the pimples, so he made a habit of checking his face in those windows. At times it seemed to Siegfried that he stood at the threshold of full manhood, so he would straighten his shoulders and flex his chest muscles. The fingers of his right hand had already wandered several times over Brunhilde's private parts, and the fingers of his left had felt her nipples. "Na," thought Siegfried in those days, "life isn't a bad business at all."

ב

AND NOW IT'S TIME TO DISCUSS SANDOR, called Gurnisht. Sandor was born to Dovid and Sureh Kleyn in a Polish town in the year in which, according to Christian chronology, the century turned over. To the midwife's great surprise, on that same day his brother Lajos also saw the light of day. At that time, in Poland, Sandor was still Shimele and Lajos was Leybl and all the neighbors said, "What beautiful babies!" and added a charm against the evil eye. They played together every day, like all other infants, in self-forgetfulness. But when they reached their fourth year, a horse stuck his head through the window frame, in the middle of the night, and neighed loudly in Lajos's ear. Lajos woke up terror stricken. Sandor also woke up in alarm, but when they took Lajos away screaming like a wild crane, he quickly went back to sleep. And because of that horse, when Lajos grew up he joined the Communists; and for this or some other reason, the Poles sacked Dovid and Sureh's house, and if they hadn't hidden in the cellar, the Poles would have done to them what they did to the chickens who were pecking in the yard at the time. That very day Dovid and Sureh packed a big sack and left town with Sandor and Lajos, at first by wagon and then by train.

When the train arrived at the outskirts of Budapest, a woman who was half Polish and half Hungarian said that in Budapest the Jews lived in Dob Utca and Sip Utca, i.e., Drum Street and Flute Street. This being the case, they went there and sold a goosedown quilt that was worth a dozen times as much in Budapest as in Poland, and they set up a stand to sell a kind of bread roll called a bagel. When Dovid found the synagogue of the Polish Jews, he began to buy chairs and tables that were getting old and sell them in the market place. So Shimele became "Sandor," Leybl became "Lajos" and Kleyn became "Kis" which means small in Hungarian. And if Lajos had not done what he had previously done in Poland, they would still be living comfortably and at peace in Sip Utca. But in nineteen hundred and nineteen the Hungarians split into Reds and Whites, and the Reds took over the government of Budapest. When Lajos saw what was happening, he rushed over to the office of the Reds, stood in front of a secretary and declared: "The Party needs me. Here I am." They immediately registered his

name. To cut a long story short, after Lajos was made an offi-
cial Communist, a Hungarian named Horty went to another
city called Szeged, gathered around him forty-seven White
generals, sent emissaries to the Romanians, to the Czechs, to
the English, and to the French, and with their help, expelled
the Reds from Budapest. When he entered the Red offices,
he found Lajos's name among other Communist names, and
ordered that he be sent to prison immediately. And although
Sandor hadn't the faintest idea what was going on, he knew
that those Hungarians that had picked up his brother would
return to look for him, so he fled his home on Sip Utca. At
first he hid in a young woman's house in Budapest, then fled
to another young woman in a Hungarian village, and finally
followed a Frenchwoman to Berlin. So Dovid and Sureh said
to themselves that for their sins the dybbuk had entered not
only Lajos, but also his twin brother Sandor who, since he
had come of age, thought only about sticking his member
into a woman's privates. In Berlin Sandor did various things
until he ran into Joseph and Yingele's place on Alexanderplatz. When he saw the gleam in their eyes, he offered himself as a tailor's apprentice. When Joseph said he had nothing
and could therefore pay nothing, Sandor was not the least bit
worried and said, "Gurnisht iz git."[1] And because he said
this, Sandor was called Gurnisht. And so Gurnisht settled
down in Joseph's house in Alexanderplatz and worked with
the needle, and when he put down the needle, he raised his
member and stuck that where he stuck it.

When Gurnisht was still in that same town in Poland he secretly held Genya's hand. And in the granary, Genya said,
"Oh. That's good, so good." His body came unto her body,

---

1. Yiddish - "Nothing is good enough."

and Genya conceived. When her father and mother saw her swollen belly they said, "Oy, what shame," and took her by wagon to a nearby city to a woman who burrowed between her legs to undo what had been done. The woman removed Gurnisht's seed from Genya's body but, together with Gurnisht's seed, absentmindedly extracted something else. When she had finished her work, the woman washed her hands and said, "Nu, the girl is Kosher again." And though Genya did not know what had happened to her, a kind of insatiable hunger entered her body, and from that day on she would succumb to any man. Because of this her father decided to send her to Palestine.

> Oy, Almighty God, just is your judgement
> There is a land that bears its sons
> In a dream, and in waking
> Buries them in the womb of its soil.

When Genya came to Palestine, an Arab with a muscular back held onto her waist and lowered her from the ship's gangplank onto the boat. When she planted her feet on the stones of the pier, and the odor of Jaffa entered her nostrils, her body forgot the snows of Poland and her blood boiled in the sun. That is why Arabs in their coffee houses stared at the curves of her legs, Jews who passed in the shade of the walls looked in her eyes, and young priests turned around to steal a quick look in daylight. And in the evening, a red sky lit the windows of the inn.

Next morning a young man sat next to Genya and told her that the olives on her plate were most certainly not to be found in Poland, while here everyone eats them. He then talked about a plot of land in Galilee where the amount of lime and moisture were well balanced and therefore he and his friends had decided to settle there and revive their ancient traditions. He then took her to the side streets of Jaffa and told her that one could tell whether an Arab came from Sudan or the Arabian desert by the bones of his cheeks. In the afternoon, he laid out Palestinian coins on the dining room table and explained to her about each coin and the Turk whose likeness was stamped on them. In the evening he took her to the seashore. At first he talked about the age of the sun and the age of the earth, and told her how the moon was simply a fragment thrown off by the earth, and the sun, which is constantly exploding, sends its rays to the earth and these rays are bounced off it to the moon which has no light of its own. Afterwards he talked about the Jews being like an inverted pyramid which could not be righted unless they came to Palestine. In another moment, Genya thought to herself, I'll turn upside down like that pyramid, and she touched his hand. The young man was quiet for a long while. Then in a different voice he asked her if she would consent to accompany him to the place in Galilee. "But," asked Genya, "will they treat me there with respect?" The young man answered, "Upon my life I swear it." And when they returned to the inn, he entered her room and said no more than was necessary.

When Genya joined the group, the other young men also talked to her about the same things, and talked with each other and disagreed about all kinds of issues and only sometimes, at night, would one or another quench the fire in her body. And once, toward evening, when the mountains of Galilee rose up like a dream dreamt by a dream, one of the men said, "This plant whose leaves are tri-labiate, is called 'Sage,' or in Latin 'Salvia triloba.'" At that moment Genya decided to leave.

When Genya left the group she went to Tiberias and lived in a guest house. To that place came Arabs who turn to Mecca, and Jews whose eyes are on Jerusalem, and Christians who stretch their necks upward, and Zionists who fix their faces on the ground. And they all found the door to her room. She lay on her back and gazed at the sky in her window. And when she was burning from the fever known as malaria, she no longer knew where she was going or whence she had come. But then her eyes cleared and she saw that the emptiness within is the same as the emptiness without, and the glass is transparent. One of her lovers bent his head and his hat tumbled into her grave.

Since Gurnisht had fled Poland in fear of the Poles, he did not know that his seed had not developed skin and bones, and that not even the tiniest tip of a finger remained to hold onto. At times, however, he imagined himself walking in the park and, on a bench, a small, dark-haired woman, and when he passes by, she lowers her eyes and says to a small boy, "Look. Here's your father."

Once a Hungarian woman with yellow hair said to Gurnisht, "Look. Here's the baby." And this story began in Budapest when they arrested his brother Lajos. At first, Gurnisht hid in the house of a Jewish woman until her father threw him out. After that he went to the house of a man called Dagadt, which in Hungarian means "Swollen," and every day he played a game of cards called Huszon Egy, which is how the Hungarians say "Twenty-one." And at sunset he went out into the streets of Budapest to look for its women. Once, while the snows of February still lay between the paving stones, he came back to Swollen's house on the last tram. As the tram arrived at one of the squares and slowed down, a young woman with yellow hair was crossing the square. Gurnisht waved his hand and, without knowing why, called after her, "What a pity. . . ." The woman turned around and smiled. This being the case, Gurnisht jumped from the tram and followed her. "I'm coming with you," he said. "You are not," she said. "Whatever happens," Gurnisht said, "I'm coming with you." "I don't mean," she said, "that I don't want you to come with me, only that I know you won't." "How," Gurnisht asked, "do you know I won't?" "When," she said, "you find out where I'm going, you won't want to come with me." "There is," Gurnisht said, "no place in the entire world that you could go to and I would not follow you." The young woman laughed and said, "We'll see." The young woman's speech was also very strange. Where Hungarians from Budapest said "O" she said "E," and where they said "E" she said "O." This, however, did not trouble Gurnisht at all. And since he had sworn to follow her to the ends of the earth, he didn't dare ask where they were going lest she think him mean-spirited. When they arrived at the Budapest railway station, the woman said, "Isn't this far enough?" But Gurnisht said, "I never go back on what I say." They traveled on the train all day, and even when they passed through countryside that Gurnisht had never seen in all his born days, he didn't ask where they were going. The young woman didn't ask his name, and said in her strange Hungarian only such things as "Let's sit here" or "It's cold" or "Here we must change trains." In the afternoon, others on the train also spoke that strange Hungarian. When they got off the train, the moon was already in the sky, and there were only a few wooden houses here and there. She walked for a long time over snow-covered fields and Gurnisht followed her. And when she came to a wooden house, she knocked on the door. An old Hungarian peeked out of the window.

When they entered, the woman pointed to Gurnisht and said, "Budapest." Gurnisht looked around and saw that there was only one room in the house for eating and sleeping. The old Hungarian said his piece, and his spouse spread out a sheet on the big bed and told Gurnisht to lie down. The young woman went to the small bed and slept there with the old Hungarian and his spouse. In the morning, when Gurnisht opened his eyes, the old man was standing by his bed with a bowl of goulash in his hand. Then he brought a bottle of milk-colored wine and Gurnisht drank until his mind became fogged. And when the Hungarian and his spouse left for the fields, the yellow-haired woman came into the big bed. Because of the wine, however, all Gurnisht remembered of the incident was the sight of one nipple and one foot. When the old man returned from the fields he put another bottle before Gurnisht. Afterwards a young Hungarian, his lower lip drooping, joined them and also drank from the bottle. The next day Gurnisht returned to Budapest. Spring soon followed. In the summer a policeman came to Swollen's house and asked after Gurnisht. When Gurnisht heard they were looking for him, he remembered the yellow-haired woman and traveled by train to her village. The old man immediately opened up a bottle of milk-colored wine. And when Gurnisht said, "I would like to stay here for a while," the old man pointed to a tool shed in the yard. In the morning Gurnisht followed the old man to the field, and in the afternoon they sat down to eat and the young Hungarian with the drooping lip joined them. All that autumn Gurnisht stayed in the old man's house and followed him and his son-in-law to the fields, and they spoke to him only when necessary. In the tenth month the yellow-haired woman gave birth to a baby girl. And when the winter winds blew, the old man went to the tool shed and called out to

Gurnisht to follow him, and he sat Gurnisht down next to the son-in-law with the drooping lip and served them wine. When Gurnisht looked out the window, he saw that the moon was full. In the middle of the night the yellow-haired woman stood before Gurnisht and said, "Look. Here's the baby." Gurnisht looked at the infant's face and saw that her lips were whole, and her face was the face of his mother Sureh. Later he returned to Budapest. At first he hid in the house of a man called "The Monkey" because of his long arms. Then he met a Frenchwoman and followed her to Berlin, and the memory of the baby faded from his mind.

When the Hungarian Circus came to Berlin, Gurnisht took Yingele by the hand and went there with him. A large horse galloped into the center of the ring. A woman with red hair stood on its back. One foot was on the horse and the other rose and fell, rose and fell. The spectators clapped, but Yingele thought to himself that God Almighty could also stand on the back of a horse. When the performance was over, Gurnisht went back to the circus wagons and kissed the red-haired woman's hand, and said something in Hungarian. At the same time, Yingele saw that the horse's back was as wide . as a table and the woman's feet were flat and thick. When they returned to Alexanderplatz, the street lights were already lit. Gurnisht put a hand on Yingele's shoulder and said, "Who's your big brother?" Yingele thought about the question a long time, and finally said, "You are." And when Yingele had gone to bed, Gurnisht wrapped a kind of green-colored scarf round his neck, twirled his moustache, and left the house. In the middle of the night Yingele heard a rustle and woke up. When his eyes adjusted to the darkness, he could see Gurnisht taking off his trousers and humming in Hungarian. "What happened?" Yingele asked. "Gurnisht," said Gurnisht. "I went to find out if that woman can also raise her legs when she is off the horse."

At times a distant image from the past comes back into Gurnisht's mind. A small town in Poland; it is Christmas. Two boys and a girl tramp through the snow carrying a box. In the box there are candles and a stage, and on the stage there are paper sheep and cows and a woman holding an infant of clay on her lap. White angel wings are sewn on the dress of the girl who is carrying the box. They stand in the doorways and sing, and the houseowners give them sweets and candy. Suddenly, between black sky and white earth, the girl stands up straight, throws the box down and says, "Screw your crippled Mother. Why should I, the angel, carry this fucking Bethlehem?" All my life, thinks Gurnisht, I've been searching for her, but I've never found anyone even half as good.

"Tell me," Gurnisht asks Joseph, "why were we expelled from the Garden of Eden?" "I've got news for you," Pomeranz the watchmaker laughs, "I was convinced we were still living in the Garden of Eden." "Don't you read the newspapers?" Kamashenmakher the matchmaker asks. "Does it say in the newspapers we were expelled?" Pomeranz asks. "It does," says the matchmaker. "If it says so, it must be true. Oy vey," says Pomeranz. Gurnisht asks again, "Why were we expelled?" "Because of our folly," Joseph says. "Our potential folly," says Gurnisht, "is made real by the spell of women." The matchmaker laughs. "The spell of women," says he, "would not have been aroused if you hadn't stood in their way." "Which proves," Pomeranz laughs, "that Gurnisht is the snake." "Doesn't he wrap himself round their bodies like a snake?" asks the matchmaker. "He does,"

Joseph says, "but there is no poison in his bite." "That," says the matchmaker, "is because he is a snake and not a schlange." "Who could give me," sighs Gurnisht, "a woman that has not eaten of the fruit of that tree?" "Because she has eaten thereof," Pomeranz says, "she can never be like one who has not." "She can vomit up the stinking fruit," says Gurnisht.

And I too, thinks Gurnisht, have that filthy fruit stuck in my throat. All my life I've been digging holes. I dig one hole, and then I dig another and fill it up with the soil I took out of the first hole.

On Purim, in the synagogue, Gurnisht covered his face and entered the women's section. When the women discovered that Gurnisht was sitting among them, they weren't angry at all, but in the synagogue itself there was a tremendous uproar and debate. The congregation split in two. There were those who argued that on Purim everyone is commanded to play the fool and there were those who argued that Purim clowning does not take precedence over the other commandments, and anyway Gurnisht acts like an old goat that just follows its lust. Gurnisht did not wait to hear what they decided, but took Yingele's hand and went to the ice-cream shop on the corner of Friedrichstrasse. And when the Polish woman who was there saw Yingele, she said, "Who is zis boy?" And Gurnisht said, "Zis is my brother." And from the ice-cream shop they went to the woman's house, and there she put a record of Polish songs on the gramophone, and Gurnisht danced in the Polish way, holding her body close to his, and over her shoulder he winked at Yingele, and Yingele winked back, though he couldn't wink with one eye.

ג

"FATHER BOUGHT A KID," JOSEPH EXPLAINS
the words of the song to Yingele, "for two marks. And the cat
came and ate the kid. And the dog came and bit the cat. And
the stick came and beat the dog. And the fire came and burnt
the stick. And the water came and put out the fire. And the
ox came and drank the water. And the butcher came and
killed the ox. And the Angel of Death came and killed the
butcher. And the Holy One, Blessed be He, came and killed
the Angel of Death that killed the butcher that killed the ox
that drank the water that put out the fire that burnt the stick
that beat the dog that bit the cat that ate the kid." And Yingele asks, "And who was left?" "The Holy one, Blessed be
He," says Joseph. "And the father," says Yingele. Joseph
hesitates a while and then adds, ". . . And the father.
. . ." Afterwards Yingele finds the afikomen under the table
cloth, and Joseph puts Yingele on his knees, and Yingele asks
for two marks in order to buy a little goat for himself. And
late in the evening, after the Passover meal, they all sing the
songs and close their eyes in pleasure. And when Yingele
begs Gurnisht to tell him one of his stories, Gurnisht recites:

> A nun lay down
> In the bed of the vicar
> The beadle came in
> And ran out quicker,
> What he told the town
> Made their joy complete:
> "I've just seen the vicar
> And he has four feet."

And, since everyone laughs, so does Yingele.

"It is Gurnisht's child," says the Polish woman from the ice-cream shop. The infant she is talking about is not really an infant, but only Gurnisht's seed embedded in her womb. And Joseph asks, "Well, what does he say?" "He says," she answers, "that I was also with Stefan. But the baby is his." "And what do you want, my child?" Joseph asks. "I don't want him to desert the baby," she says. And after a moment's silence she adds, "and the mother." "And what," Joseph asks, "do your family say?" "I am alone in this world," she says. Joseph gets up from his chair and makes tea, and the woman sips from the cup, and Yingele sees beads of sweat on her forehead. "And what about Stefan?" Joseph asks. "He wants to marry me," she says. "And you," Joseph asks, "Don't you love him?" "I do," she says, "but I love Gurnisht more." And Yingele remembers Purim when Gurnisht went into the women's section and there was an uproar in the synagogue, and that was why Gurnisht went to the Polish woman's house and pressed her body close to his body and winked at him over her shoulder. "I see, sir," she says, "that you are quite attached to your son." "Gurnisht," Joseph says, "is a good man, but he cannot bring a woman happiness." The woman fixes her blue eyes on the tailor's table. "Would you agree, sir," she says, "to talk to Stefan for me?" And when Stefan comes in, Joseph holds out his hand to him and Stefan sits down at the table, and Joseph takes a bottle of Kiddush wine out of the cupboard and pours some for Stefan, and Stefan looks at Joseph with blue eyes and says, "To your health, Sir," and reports that at present he is still a carpenter's apprentice, but the shopowner has promised next year, Lord willing, to make him a quarter partner. And Stefan goes on to say that the woman is from his hometown and dear to him, but that the "gentleman's assistant" is turning her head. Joseph promises that the assistant will not go near her again, and thrusts twenty marks into Stefan's hand for "wedding expenses."

> Behold, thou art fair, my love
> In the ice-cream shop
> Behold, thou art fair,
> With blue eyes like doves
>
> Behold, thou art fair, my beloved—
> Yea, pleasant.
> Thy hair as black as a raven,
> Also our bed is green.
>
> Behold, Stefan standeth
> Behind our wall
> He looketh forth at the windows
> Showing himself through the lattice
>
> Rise up, my love, in the ice-cream shop
> For, lo, the winter is past
> The flowers appear on the earth
> Rise up, and come away
>
> A time to embrace and a time to refrain from
>   embracing
> A time to get and a time to lose
> A time to keep and a time to cast away
> A time to rend and a time to sew

And, when the matter of the Polish woman is settled, Gurnisht meets a German woman with pale eyes and skin as pure as marble. Gurnisht wants to set the water on fire, and hits the bottle all day long. In the middle of the night, he comes to her house and prostrates himself before her. And the German woman's body is drawn to her soul, and her soul blazes like steel. Completely flawless, she nevertheless lusts after a tailor's apprentice from Alexanderplatz whose hair is black and whose eyes are green. Gurnisht's forehead is wet and he exhales wine fumes. He whispers, "Come, Brigitte, my impossible one." And he squeezes the space between his body and her body, and the space is pushed out to the sides, and Brigitte's nipples feel cold against Gurnisht's chest. And when I come, Gurnisht thinks, I'll be delivered from death. And what does Brigitte's head think on the lace pillow her mother embroidered on those autumn and winter evenings, when Brigitte's father sat in his armchair? It thinks, "this is not bad." And it also thinks, "this is quite nice." And that is why Gurnisht's body cannot enter the marble temple. When he leaves, Brigitte's face is seen in the window like the bust of a dead composer.

And the pillar of fire in his body leads him to the gypsy camp on the outskirts of Berlin. A dark-skinned man with gold rings on his fingers pours him wine. "Romanian," says the dark one. "Hungarian," says Gurnisht. "We are brothers," they both say and fall into each other's arms. Then the dark man embraces Gurnisht and leads him to a wooden wagon. "This is my brother," he says, "be good to him, Rozsi." And Rozsi, who could be a woman or a girl, raises the edge of her blanket and Gurnisht's pillar of fire enters her. Flame devours flame, and sounds of sighing. Lice are burnt up. Shadows dance on the ceiling.

And thus was written
In the police files:
Arrested. Not Aryan. At dawn.

A drunkard that claims he fell
In a frozen lake and rose
From it in a
Burning railway coach.
Fined twenty
Marks and warned.

And even though his eyes were black and not green like Gurnisht's, in those days Yingele's eyes also captured the heart of a German woman. That's why she offers him a suger-coated roll and says, "a sweet roll for a sweet boy." And when Yingele leaves half of the roll on the park bench, the woman tells him that Kaspar didn't want to finish his soup, and so he became thin and died. And when Yingele puts his thumb in his mouth, she tells him about Konrad who sucked his thumb and so the tailor came with a big pair of scissors and—klick-klack—cut off both of Konrad's thumbs.

When Yingele returns to Alexanderplatz, he asks Gurnisht if they buried Kaspar in the ground and what happened to Konrad's thumbs that were cut off. And when Gurnisht asks who Kaspar and Konrad are, Yingele tells him. But Gurnisht says that neither Kaspar nor Konrad ever existed, but are only characters in a German story, just like Hänsel and Gretel who were eaten by a witch.

Then Gurnisht becomes a highwayman and Yingele holds an imaginary sword over him. Gurnisht grabs his chest with his fists and falls on his face. "I'm dead," Gurnisht says. And when the odor of the wood floor enters his nostrils, Gurnisht imagines he is lying in a forest among the roots of pine trees. Yingele calls out his name, but Gurnisht lies in silence without moving. And when Yingele bursts into tears, Gurnisht wishes Joseph also to come and cry. But he reaches out his hand from under his stomach and grabs Yingele's heel. Then he turns over on his back and presses Yingele to his heart until Yingele laughs. "I thought," says Yingele, his eyes still full of tears, "that Gurnisht was dead."

In nineteen hundred and thirty-three, in July, the bees sucked nectar from the flowers in the Berlin parks. And even though he had been explicitly asked not to set foot in those places reserved for Germans, Gurnisht, whose eyes were green rather than black, found himself in a coffeehouse on Wilhelmstrasse.

The women that walk up and down Wilhelmstrasse, thinks Gurnisht to himself, have their chins set on marble columns, chin after chin, each with its column. And they walk along the avenue, their hands holding the columns and their eyes hard. "My chin is on my column," their faces say, "and my column is in my hand." They are here at ten-thirty and there at five-thirty, and their "ja" is short and to the point, and so is their "nein." Gurnisht remembers the market women in Hungary with downy beards on their cheeks, who grab hold of the genitals of the farmers. "Well, Methuselah, can you still stick it in?" When the Messiah comes to the world, Gurnisht thinks, he will first go to Berlin and stick his finger in the vaginas of the women who stroll in their hats down Wilhelmstrasse until their "ja" and "nein" fall into disarray and their marble columns shatter. What will they do then, chins exposed to the light of the world? With the finger of the Messiah between their legs, will they say, "Please, Herr Messiah, return the column on which my chin stood?" "In memory of the Temple," he will say. "In memory of the Temple."

In the afternoon the shade from the café's awning made way for the sun which fell on the face of a young woman. A fly that had dipped first in the apple strudel flew up and stood on a tiny drop of sweat, as clear as crystal, on the woman's nose.

The woman waved her delicate hand in front of her face and said in an extended melody at first precise and then, like a siren, lower and lower: "Fl.............y." And when this melody fell on Gurnisht's ears, his soul took flight and hovered over the café's awning, and from there it saw that the woman was English and her skin was rose-colored, and her hair like honey.

And when his soul returned, Gurnisht sat himself down next to the Englishwoman and learned from her that her name was Elizabeth. And even before they left, Elizabeth had fallen in love with Gurnisht and made up her mind to stay with him. And Gurnisht, too, whose spirit in those days was still reeling between fire and water, wanted to rest his head in her lap. And even more than he yearned to smell the odor of soap given off by Elizabeth, Gurnisht yearned to roam the streets of London, whose citizens are known for their good manners, and never expel anyone from their coffeehouses.

When Gurnisht stood before Joseph his spirit sank and he thought, "How can I live elsewhere, without Joseph and without Yingele?" But Joseph, who saw what he saw, said, "It seems it's time for you to go away." And Gurnisht, who could not bear to look into Yingele's eyes, took the golden dwarf with horns on his head from his neck, put it on a chair next to Yingele's bed, and left the house on Alexanderplatz in the dead of night.

When Gurnisht arrived in London he stayed at first in a guest house in Whitechapel, and couldn't pluck up courage to eat anything except cooked carrots, until he was invited to visit Elizabeth at home. When he arrived he discovered that her father, Mr. Fred Goldstone, was none other than Froyke Goldsteyn who had come to London after the Great War from a Hungarian town called Bekasmegyer and hired himself out to a Scottish tailor named McGregor, and succeeded so well in the tailoring business that he became the Scot's partner and they called the business "McGregor and Goldstone." And when Fred Goldstone found out that Gurnisht was Sandor Kis who was none other than Shimele Kleyn, his eyes watered and they both hummed Hungarian songs. And when the maids cleared the table, Froyke took Shimele's hand, and they both danced the Csardas.

So Fred Goldstone gave Gurnisht the delicate hand of his daughter Elizabeth, and brought him into the tailoring business. And though there was still a glint of fire in Gurnisht's eyes, he accustomed himself to Elizabeth's body, and would come and go between the father-in-law's business and the daughter's house. And all because of a fly in Berlin.

ז

EVEN THOUGH IT WOULD BE BETTER TO stay in Berlin and tell about Joseph and Yingele, it is necessary to talk first about Lajos, Gurnisht's brother, who remained in Hungary. Lajos has nothing to do with our story or with any other story, but since his body was coupled to

Gurnisht's body before birth, it would be improper to talk
about one and ignore the other.

Lajos himself wrote down most of the things that happened
to him. He did this so that his deeds would not, God forbid,
be wiped out of human memory. From what he wrote down,
one could fill three thick volumes, and what will be told here
is a mere drop in the ocean. Yet that drop is amazingly similar
to the reservoir from which it came.

From the court transcript:

September 21, 1923

Prosecutor: Your revolution of 1919 served Russia's, not
    Hungary's, goals.
Lajos: In 1919 the Hungarian people rose up in arms. The
    blood of the Hungarian workers and the Russian workers
    was spilled and mingled for the sacred goal of the Socialist
    Revolution. Lenin remarked on the Hungarian workers'
    Revolution of 1919—
Prosecutor: We are not—
Lajos: The next workers' Revolution will be the glorious
    continuation of 1919—
Prosecutor: I am calling you to order—
Lajos: As Comrade Rakosi has already said, and I agree with
    every word, the workers will shatter—
Prosecutor: That will be sufficient!
Lajos: And the Hungarian Counter-Revolution will fail—
Prosecutor: Enough!
Lajos: The Young Workers' Movement that was founded at
    the Conference—
Prosecutor: Sit down!
Lajos: —Lenin . . .

From the Diary of Lajos Kis

December 17, 1923

This week they put Grinblat in the cell. He disguises himself as a Communist, but he is a Trotskyite. He is short, thin, dark and his hair stands up like the spines of a hedgehog. I thought, "He looks exactly like an agent-provocateur." Grinblat is a foreign body in our midst, and everyone is giving him the silent treatment.

February 2, 1924

The prosecutor called in our neighbor, Gros, for interrogation and asked him about me. He is fat and never suspected that the son of Dovid and Sureh was a revolutionary. His wife had hinted to me several times that they would be happy to give me their daughter's hand. She is sixteen years old, and studies at the Lycée. I thought, "There is no room for marriage in my life."

March 13, 1924

I read Zakuski's book, "Towards the Light, Brothers," in the toilet. It's a Soviet novel about the red Cossacks in the 1919 Revolution. When I received the book, I ripped off the cover and tore the book into several parts so that it would look like toilet paper. I thought, "An unforgettable book."

August 17, 1924

Yesterday they put some street women here. This is a political prison, but apparently there's a shortage of prison cells. They put them in the next cell. I didn't see them, but I heard their voices. One of them shouted, "How long is your——?

Why don't you drill a hole in the wall and stick your——into our cell?" I thought, "In a socialist society, it will be our duty to educate these women to productive labor."

May 22, 1926

The first issue of the Hungarian Communist Party's journal, "New March," has just come out in Moscow. Declarations of solidarity from San Francisco, Sydney, Reykjavik. Also from Peking: "The Chinese workers stand behind Rakosi Matyas and his comrades." I thought, "Far away in China, a coolie gave a cent to the struggle and so went without cigarettes or didn't go to the cinema."

October 1, 1926

Today for lunch they gave us potatoes with cabbage. Undercooked. I wrote a complaint to the prison warden. Stalin's latest speech on the five-year plan appeared in "New March." Heavy industry has already saved 30 million rubles. I thought, "Long live the Revolution!"

January 7, 1929

My mother came to visit today. She cried the whole time. I thought, "My mother has never understood my ideals." She brought me a bagel. I gave half to Rakosi. I sleep on a mattress, but he doesn't have even that.

Sureh Kleyn's letter to her son Lajos Kis

January 8, 1929

When I visited you in prison yesterday, I cried and couldn't speak, so now your mother is writing this letter to you. My

Leybl, I didn't cry because you are in prison, although no one in our family has ever been in prison before. Before I came to you I had decided not to cry, but to tell you everything that is happening on Sip Utca just as if we were chatting at home. But you, Leybl, my dearest son, looked at me with such cold eyes that I had to cry. Where did I sin, my Leybl? Don't tell me I'm mistaken because I know that look. When you were a child I always cared for you, even more than for your brother Shimele. What did your father and I do to you? Your father is not the same person. He comes home from the synagogue and his face is yellow. And every Sabbath he sits and does not talk. Even when they almost killed us all in Poland, he was not like this. He has no joy from his sons, poor man. One son is in prison and the other chases women (also shiksehs) all the time. He never complains, God forbid, but only sighs, "Oy vey," and I have to be strong for both of us. Do you think the goyim thank you for what you are doing for them? Last week a policeman came again to ask all kinds of questions about your friends and your brother, and the neighbors have been whispering. Oy, what shame! Leybl, my dearest son, didn't you see yesterday that it was me, your mother, sitting before you? Don't think that your father doesn't come because he is angry with you. He has no more strength. He no longer goes to the market, only to the synagogue, and all our income now comes from my bagels. Was the bagel that I brought tasty? The glaze on top was made from sugar, eggs, and a little honey. First you heat them, and when they cool you spread the glaze on with a brush. Your mother's invention. Leybl, I know you are brave. But it is not bravery to look at your mother like that. I know you didn't mean it, but don't think your friends love you more than your father and mother.

From the Diary of Lajos Kis

April 17, 1929

Rakosi received a letter from Moscow. I looked at the envelope for a long time. On the six-kopeck stamp, a factory worker. On the twenty-kopeck stamp, a farmer. The enemies of the Revolution have not succeeded in isolating the Soviet Union from the world. The stamps cross frontiers, bringing tidings from the Russian worker and farmer. On the back of the envelope is stamped: "We shall finish the five-year plan in four years." I thought, "Finish it, Russian brothers, finish it."

July 20, 1934

They took me to the infirmary. Stomach pains. On my side, next to the wall, a Czech with an artificial leg. About sixty years old. Pleasant fellow. Murdered his wife. After him, a Jew with short hair who argues all the time with his neighbor, a strict Catholic, who claims that Jesus was a Hungarian. He snores at night. Then me. And next to the wall there is a Slovak who says he didn't steal any chickens, but they arrested him because he is a Slovak. On the far side, next to the wall, a gypsy who is dying. Next to him a worker from heavy industry. He tried to break into the warehouse because of his meager salary. A promising youngster. Then comes the pail (our toilet) and after that a thief who killed two people. Next to the wall there is a tiler with one kidney. In the evening I talked about the Revolution.

May 2, 1936

Last week I found a piece of iron in the garbage and carved the Soviet star on my bed. Four of the points turned out well, and only the fifth point was too wide. I developed blisters from so much work. I thought, "It was worth it."

And in 1937 a Hungarian delegate secretly visited a Russian delegate and said, "If you return to us the sword of the Hungarian hero Kossuth, that your Czar took with him to Moscow in 1848, we shall give you, in exchange, all the Communists that are sitting in our prisons." And when the news reached Stalin he thought what he thought and said, "So be it." And when the Hungarian Communists arrived in Moscow, they fell down and kissed the asphalt of the railway station. Stalin was unable to sleep. He got up in the middle of the night, called someone and said, "Tomorrow, the Hungarians." And as they were leading Lajos to the gallows, he shouted, "I am not a Trotskyite agent." "That's right," said the hangman, "you're a capitalist dog."

> At first
> Lajos' descent looked
> quite promising.
> Why did he stop
> fifty-three centimeters
> above the ground?

Greater than the miracle that men exist, Joseph thinks, is the miracle that they have faces. The miracle that they exist never changes, but the miracle that they have faces is ever new. For the face of Solomon, there is the miracle of Solomon's face; for the face of Pomeranz, there is the miracle of Pomeranz's face. And if Gurnisht did not have the face of Gurnisht, the place where his face had been, Joseph thinks, would not now be so empty. And on his chest Yingele wears a dwarf with horns on his head and wishes the face of someone like Gurnisht would take the place of Gurnisht's face, but when he sees a man who resembles Gurnisht, he can't help turning away. Once a man shows his face to another, Yingele thinks, and a link is formed between spirit and face, he should not be permitted to take his face away. And the photographs a person leaves behind are not enough for consolation. It would have been better to go away without leaving any trace, so that people would not have to look, day and night, in other faces for the face they have lost.

And Joseph understands what is in Yingele's heart and tells jokes, at times, like Gurnisht did. But Joseph's jokes are like Joseph's face, and when he says things that Gurnisht used to say, there is, underneath, a certain sadness.

As the years went by Chaya-Leah's face receded, and when Joseph tries to recall her appearance he can see her only through a cloud of fog. But sometimes her face comes to him and appears for a moment in the face of Yingele. In the winter, when there are snowflakes on the windowpanes of Berlin, Joseph sees the winds that blow in the forest and across the frozen plains. Old odors return to his nose. Then he imagines that what has happened was only a dream, and that he is now sitting, as he did every evening, sewing stockings and Chaya-Leah is sitting at his side. But when he wakes from his daydream, Joseph sees the fear in Yingele's eyes, and realizes he was speaking to Chaya-Leah.

At night Joseph puts his hand on Yingele's stomach and tells him that Yingele was in Chaya-Leah's stomach nine months until his organs were fully grown. And Yingele imagines he

is tiny as a pin and lies inside his mother's stomach, and
Joseph puts his hand on Chaya-Leah's stomach, and that is
why his limbs grow and grow until he becomes a real child.

ה

SIEGFRIED TOOK A CANDLE FROM THE
drawer of the kitchen table. He lit the wick, dripped wax into
a soup bowl, and fixed the bottom of the candle in the bowl.
Then he placed the bowl on the chair next to his bed. His
body cast a shadow on the ceiling. He knelt down next to the
bed and held his breath. When the first one appeared,
Siegfried raised his hand and crushed it against the edge of
the bed. The second one dodged the first blow, but when
Siegfried hit it the second time its blood smeared on the wall.
Siegfried killed the third one on the floor. He scraped the
dead bug off the wall and carefully placed it next to the one
on the edge of the bed. Then he picked up the dead bug from
the floor and put it next to the others. Then Siegfried covered
himself with his blanket and looked at the bugs on the edge
of the bed until the candle went out.

More than Yingele wanted to see Chaya-Leah's face, he
yearned to touch her body. When the daughter of Solomon,
the butcher, handed him a chicken, Yingele reached up
higher than necessary, and his hand touched her hand. But
Rebecca Solomon's fingers were raw and her skin cold.
Solomon wrung the chicken's neck and plucked its feathers.
And when it lay spread out on the table, Yingele touched it.
Its flesh was still warm and its skin smooth and soft. From
the dismembered head the eyes, half closed, stared at the
naked body.

But at night, Joseph hugs Yingele, and Yingele plants his feet on Joseph's stomach. They pull the blanket over their heads, and the darkness inside becomes a cave, and outside a man-eating wolf lies in wait for Yingele, and Joseph raises the edge of the blanket and lets the wolf stick its snout into the opening of the cave. And Yingele shouts with excitement and presses close to Joseph's body until Joseph blocks up the opening and saves Yingele from the wolf's claws. And at the same time, Joseph's soul almost faints from pleasure, and he too imagines himself a baby in his mother's womb. When Yingele tires of these games and his eyes glaze over, he asks Joseph to put a hand on his stomach and tell him a story. Joseph wants to tell him Bible stories, but Yingele quickly tires of such stories, and when Joseph begins with "The children of Israel" or "Moses," he asks for a different story. So Joseph racks his brains and tells Yingele the story of the flood, but is careful not to mention Noah by name. And when Joseph tells about the animals that went into the ark, Yingele asks "and what about the birds?" "and the leopards?" "and the wolves?" Yingele likes this story a lot and compels Joseph to give the animals names. And Joseph gives the birds and the squirrels the names of people he remembers from his hometown; to the wolves and the lions he gives names of Russians; and to the dogs and the hyenas he gives names of Germans. In a frivolous moment, Joseph calls the cat "Yingele," and from then on Yingele wants to know if the cat was large or small, and what color was its fur and what did it do in the ark and where was it when the dove returned to the ark with an olive leaf in its mouth and, when the waters receded, was it the first to leave the ark. One day Joseph realized that Herr Schultz, who had ordered a suit made from English cloth, appeared in his mind's eye as a jackal.

When Joseph walks the old streets of Berlin, he remembers Uncle Pinye who sank into melancholy in the year that the century turned over. When Joseph was a child, Uncle Pinye lived in the attic. In the evenings he would stick his head out of the window and blow a shofar. A loud wail would spread across the plains and its echo would roll back from the forest. "To hasten the coming of the Messiah," Reb Khayim would justify his brother upstairs. And when Joseph saw hunters on the path leading to the forest, he imagined that they too were moving under the influence of the blasts of his Uncle Pinye.

Uncle Pinye's image has faded from Joseph's memory, but when he sees the attics on Potsdamstrasse, he recalls the forest smells and the sounds of broken weeping. Then Joseph thinks, without knowing why, "In Berlin, Redemption has drawn nearer."

Siegfried was very happy when Karl taught him the song. "It's a long time since I heard such a good song," he thought. When he recited the words to Brunhilde, she said, "Don't be such a fool," but Siegfried thought, "What a blockhead. All her brains are between her legs." When he got home, his father was sitting in the kitchen drinking fusel.[1] "I know a song," Siegfried said. "And that bastard," his father was saying to Gertrud, "had the nerve to tell me, 'if you do that, they'll fire you' as if butter wouldn't melt in his mouth." "Everybody else knows better," Gertrud said. "Listen to a song," Siegfried said to Gertrud's little daughter:

1. A cheap German cognac.

Herr von Ha-gen
Dürft ich Wa-gen
Sie zu fra-gen
Wieviel Kra-gen
Sie getra-gen
Als sie la-gen
Krank im Ma-gen
In der Hauptstadt
Kopenha-gen[1]

And when Joseph brought the trousers he had sewn for Fritz Bohme to his house on Bismarckstrasse, Herr Bohme set himself down on a chair and took off his old trousers. And Joseph saw that a carpenter had once held a chisel and carved there, on the chair, lion paws. Then Herr Bohme put on the trousers Joseph had sewn, placed himself in front of the mirror, stared at Herr Bohme and said, "Zum Teufel.[2] I didn't order such trousers." "Ober . . ."[3] Joseph said. "Nein," said Herr Bohme, "I ordered different trousers. Guten Tag." When Joseph left with Herr Bohme's trousers, it was spring on Bismarckstrasse and there were birds in the treetops. Joseph sat down on a bench and thought about men's souls, how each soul has a holy sphere, but below it, at the very bottom where it emerges into the world, every man has the spirit of an animal. Sometimes this spirit is like a bird that hops from branch to branch, singing to its heart's content, and sometimes it is like a bull that butts and gores when its fury drives it mad. So Joseph Silverman sat on the bench on Bismarckstrasse and thought about the Sphere known as

1. German - Mr. von Ha-gen/ May I ask/ How many collars you wore/ When you were in bed/ With a stomachache/ In the capital city of/ Copenhagen.
2. German - "Damn it."
3. Yiddish - "But . . ."

"Malchut," or Majesty, which is the revealed world. And from that sphere his thoughts were drawn to other spheres, and his soul climbed ever upward until it reached the sphere of "Nothingness" from which all worlds emanate. Meanwhile, the king or emperor of one of Europe's nations was passing through Bismarckstrasse, dragging behind him a trail of officers and bigwigs. That's why a great crowd had gathered—men, women and children—and they all started cheering in honor of the king. When one of the king's guards saw that everyone was standing and cheering, and only a thick-bearded man, with one pair of trousers on his legs and another pair hanging down on both sides of his knees, was sitting gazing at the treetops, he went to Joseph and asked, "Why aren't you standing in honor of the king?" Then he searched Joseph's clothes, and when he found a pair of scissors in his pocket, he called to his comrade and they both took Joseph to the guard house. When they arrived at the guard house, they put Joseph's scissors on the officer's desk and talked among themselves about people called anarchists who have thick beards and wander about Europe shooting kings and princes, and stabbing them with knives and other sharp instruments. And since it was a Friday and the sun was beginning to set, Joseph Silverman asked only to be allowed to return home before the Sabbath eve. And because he spoke Yiddish and flung out his arms and kept on repeating "Shabes, Shabes," these same officers were of the opinion that he had secretly come from Bulgaria. And if a Jewish German who spoke to Joseph in broken Yiddish and to the officers in perfect German had not chanced by, they would not have allowed him to return to his home on Alexanderplatz before the Sabbath eve.

"If my forefathers had not mixed with such distinguished circles," Herr Cohn says to Joseph, "they would not have changed their name." Herr Cohn's ancestors had arrived in Germany during the eighteenth century and in those days, when their name was still Cohen, they bought horses and sold them to the farmers of Bavaria. But Herr Cohn's grandfather became a counsellor to a German prince and settled in Berlin, and when he died he left Herr Cohn's father much property and a new name without the "e."

Names, Joseph thinks, are strange. For instance, the man who ordered striped trousers—you can see from his face that the sights he sees give him pleasure, yet his name is Sorgen.[1] Whereas the man who sits at the loan counter in the "Industrial Bank," with his head tilted to one side as though expecting some catastrophe to occur at any moment, is called Sorgenfrei.[2]

Once, Joseph remembers, a man with a large corporation came into his shop, bowed and said, "Störich,"[3] and Gurnisht said, "No." The man repeated "Störich" and again Gurnisht said, "No. Certainly not." This kept up until it turned out that "Störich" was the man's name. The man, however, took no offense and told a story about a man who introduced himself by the name of "Sauerkraut." "I beg your pardon?" the other man said. "Sauerkraut" the man repeated a second time. "I'm sorry," the other one said, "Say it again please." "Sauerkraut" the man repeated for the third time. "You probably won't believe this," the other one said, "but I keep on hearing 'Sauerkraut.'" And Gurnisht who liked the story a great deal, burst out laughing and he too told a story

1. German - Worrier.
2. German - Worry-free.
3. German (Stör' ich) - "I disturb."

about a butcher called Ochsenkopf[1] and a doctor that specialized in the urinary canals whose name was Pischnot.[2] When the beginning of someone's name, for example, is "Von," Gurnisht said, everyone immediately treats him with the greatest respect. That's why, he said, I'm going to change my name to "Von Gurnisht."

When Herr Cohn's father died, all his great wealth passed into the hands of Herr Cohn, who had one daughter whom he wished Joseph Silverman to marry. "Even though you are not a German," Herr Cohn said to Joseph, "you are a Jew like me. You are devoted to your son. But the boy can not go on," Herr Cohn said, "without a mother." And when Herr Cohn's daughter came to the shop, Joseph saw that she was addressing the tailor's dummy, so he did not answer her. But when he listened to what she was saying and heard her ask to take Herr Cohn's trousers home, Joseph realized she was not talking to the dummy, but to him and that her eyes, which were looking at the dummy, were seeing him. There's nothing wrong with that, Joseph thought to himself, for the eyes of a woman to look at one place and see another, as long as her soul is chaste and her manner gentle. And Joseph saw how Yingele looked at other children and thought about their mothers, who sit and wait for them to come home and, when they arrive, stroke their hair and ask them if they would like a dumpling. Heaven has decreed, Joseph thinks, that I should be a poor tailor, but I have not yet brought my son, whom I saved from murderers, to a safe haven. And here we are nothing but phantoms which the German sees in his sleep; he says to himself, "When I awake I will see that these were

1. German - Ox-head.
2. German - Urinary distress.

but creatures of my dream." That's why Yingele does not learn the language of the German as it should be spoken, but only a little bit here and a little bit there. And the melamed[1] in the cheder[2] has nothing of his own except his poverty and his dead alphabet, and all of us wander about like shadows. But Herr Cohn, Joseph thinks, although not the same kind of Jew as us, is nevertheless a Jew, and knows the language of the German and his customs, and maybe his soul will embrace Yingele's soul, and he will do for him what a grandfather can do for his grandson, which I am powerless to do.

Joseph therefore yields to Herr Cohn's pressing invitations to visit him at the "coffee hour." And the house is situated in a different neighborhood of Berlin where not just anybody can enter, but rather one must first stand before a doorkeeper who asks the houseowner if he would be so pleased as to consider seeing a visitor. And in Herr Cohn's drawing room, which is darkened by heavy curtains, a large cupboard towers to the ceiling, and inside its glass doors silver vessels stand like knights on the turrets of a fortress.

And when Herr Cohn's daughter talks to Joseph she looks at Yingele, and when she talks to Yingele she looks at Joseph, but Yingele talks to her as though her eyes were looking at him. In the house on Alexanderplatz Yingele takes what he wants, and after the meal says one thank-you for everything he has received. But in Herr Cohn's house, the meal is divided into chapters and the chapters into verses and one gives thanks after each verse. Herr Cohn's daughter therefore teaches Yingele to say "Dankeschön" when they move

---

1. A Bible teacher for small Jewish children.
2. Melamed's classroom.

his chair close to the table, and "Dankeschön" when they serve him cake on a plate, and "Dankeschön" when they pour a drink into his glass. Yingele's body is hidden by the height of the table and only his head fills the space between the cake and the apple juice.

After the coffee, Herr Cohn talks about the Jews from the East who, because of the troubled times, have not acquired "Kultur" like the Jews of Germany. And Herr Cohn's daughter asks Joseph who his customers are, and Joseph chooses to talk about Solomon, the butcher, and Pomeranz, the watchmaker, and does not mention others like the judge Höhenzoller or Herr Doktor Fröhlich. And Herr Cohn's daughter squeezes her thighs together and purses her lips as if to say, "I like the tailor well enough, and it's possible to educate the boy, but a self-respecting woman would not be seen dead in a place where there are Pomeranzes and Solomons." And Joseph remembers Chaya-Leah and thinks to himself that it is better to have Chaya-Leah without Kultur than Kultur without Chaya-Leah. And as for Herr Cohn's daughter, Joseph thinks, where is this treasure of hers which she desires to share with another—I can't see it. And how could I make her happy? She would be better off married to a Jew who is also a German, and can understand her. The business of her eyes is not really a problem, such a man would quickly learn what her eyes see, wherever she looks. And now that I know how the Germans divide their meals into chapter and verse and give thanks at the end of each verse, I can see to it myself that Yingele behaves properly.

When Joseph returns to Alexanderplatz and explains that what might have happened between himself and Herr

Cohn's daughter is not going to happen, Pomeranz says, "A fool sees a woman's reflection in the water and drinks up the whole lake. Go and say 'Goymel Bentshn.'[1]" And Kamashenmakher, the matchmaker, laughs and says, "Instead of being married off to someone like that, better to marry Fride the meshigene."[2]

"They were lovely and pleasant in their lives," Fride sings, "and in their deaths they were not divided." "Who are you talking about, Fride?" Pomeranz asks. "About monkeys," Fride says, "about monkeys. When the female paints her behind, the male knows that his time has come." And Fride, who is also wearing a flowered dress, alternately laughs and cries.

On sunny days, Fride leans against the stone wall in Alexanderplatz, holds on to the coat sleeves of passersby and says, "Where are you going?" "Where are you going?" "Where are you going?" No one knows how she arrived in Berlin. And Fride herself remembers only what happened before she came. In Kopichuk, in Lithuania, she loved a boy named Moshe and he loved her, and they swore to be faithful to each other. And when the Great War broke out the Russians sent Moshe to the battlefield, and Fride went to Wilkomir with her father and mother, who wished to distance themselves from the contending armies. And there, in Wilkomir, they urged her to marry another man, but Fride, who remembered her vow to Moshe, refused. And after the war, when Fride returned to Kopichuk, she found Moshe married to another woman. And when that woman gave birth to a

---

1. Yiddish - Prayer of Thanksgiving for escape from danger.
2. Yiddish - The mad one.

stillborn child, Moshe went to Fride and begged her to for-
give him and remove the spell of evil eye. But by then, Fride
had no understanding of other minds, her own mind stood
apart and both her eyes were fixed on the roots of the world.
"The baby," Fride said, "is mine, that I laid in your nest and
you wrapped in silken threads and gave to that harlot that
she would lie with you, and as she lay with you, she ate the
baby up." And everyone believed that because of Fride's
curse, Moshe's wife, from then on, cooked only noodle soup,
called Youkh mit Lokshn. After a year, Moshe got fed up
with his wife's soup, threw the bowl through the window, left
the house and disappeared without a trace. And perhaps
Fride was looking for him in Berlin.

Joseph serves Fride tea. "You," Fride says to Joseph, "are a
good man, but he," as she points to Pomeranz, "abandoned
me to my sighs." "Not me, Fride," Pomeranz says, "it was
another man. In another place." "In another place?" Fride
says, "And where is here?" "Here," Pomeranz says, "is
Berlin." "Berlin?" Fride says. "Berlin," Pomeranz says, "of
the Germans." "And the Germans," asks Fride, "abandon
their wives?" Pomeranz shrugs his shoulders. "The Germans," he says, "do everything with complete thoroughness,
which they call 'gründlich,' whether they abandon their
wives or not." And for some reason Pomeranz's answer satis-
fies Fride, and she says, "Birds too hatch from trees."

But when Fride returns to the musty smells of her room, her
head splits in two, and bursts with the din. In the Lithuanian
Fride a host of choirs congregate and break out in song,
"Trees, Trees, Trees," while opposed to them, choirs of the
Berlin Fride respond with "Eggs, Eggs, Eggs." And when
the controversy is not settled by fugal means, regiment after

regiment inside the Lithuanian Fride revel in the music of
the Passion while in the Berlin Fride an enormous crowd op-
poses them with the trumpet blasts of the Requiem:

> Vanity of vanities,
>> In February the waters freeze.
>
> All is vanity
>> Ravens fall down dead from trees.
>
> What profit hath a man
>> Peter won't do what he's told,
>
> Of all his labor under the sun
>> Wears spring clothes, although it's cold
>
> Generations come and go
>> Hunters find him frozen stiff
>
> But the earth abideth for ever
>> Mother sobs, prostrate with grief
>
> The sun rises and the sun sets
>> Father says, "He was so nice"
>
> And returns to where it rises
>> But Peter's now a block of ice.
>
> Ever turning blows the wind
>> Though they bring it near the heat
>
> On its rounds the wind returns
>> Peter's gone, his death's complete.
>
> All streams flow into the sea
>> Melted, all it yields is rather
>
> Yet the sea is never full.
>> Less than a plate of soup for Father.

At the New Year, at the time of the longest blast on the shofar, Fride broke the glass window in the women's gallery of
the synagogue. When the worshippers held on to her and led

her outside, Solomon the butcher placed one finger on his forehead and declared, "Meshigene." Solomon was wearing a blue suit and around his neck was a prayer-shawl woven with threads of gold. But on other days he would stick his hand into the innards of chickens, and the apron around his stomach would be splattered with bloodstains. And when Klein's photography shop was on fire and everyone gathered around and cried out, "Water" or "Buckets" or "Break down the door," Fride the insane waved her arms in the air and laughed. And when Joseph also looked where she was looking, he saw the bride and groom in Klein's front window. Their chins were burning and their faces smiled.

The women on Auguststrasse stand in the doorways and drop all kinds of hints. When a man looks them in the face, they entice him with words. Some speak as though they cannot be denied, others are full of entreaty. "Come here, my prince of dreams," they say, "come, let us make love." And to Joseph's ears the voices sound, at times, like a melody of prayer. Women, Joseph thinks, yearn to embrace a man, and a man yearns to embrace his Creator, as the verse says: "I sought him, but I could not find him; I called him, but he gave me no answer." And both pleas wander side by side in empty space. Joseph's heart pines for those voices, he would like to follow them, but his feet carry him, against his will, to Herr Schloss's fabric shop. On his way back to Alexanderplatz he carries a roll of cloth on his shoulder, and takes another route, where there is nothing special to be seen, and all is profane.

In December, when the gentiles celebrated the birth of God, Joseph went to Auguststrasse and thought, "On my bed." "By night on my bed," he thought, "by night on my bed I sought him whom my soul loveth." "Komm," the

women said. "Komm." A white mist rose from their lips.
"As the heart panteth after the water brooks," Joseph
thought, "so panteth my soul after thee." "Komm," the
women whispered, "Komm." "My soul thirsteth," "Komm"
"Komm" "for the living God." And he went with a woman
and knew her. And he went to the fabric shop and loaded a
roll of cloth on his back, and on his way home he saw that all
the other streets were full of sights, and all was holy.

ו

WHEN IT WAS ANNOUNCED ON THE RADIO
and in the newspapers about "Strength through Joy,"[1]
Siegfried went to pave the autobahn. So did Karl, and even
Kurt Becker, though everyone disliked him. When the asphalt was poured and they were spreading it with rakes, Kurt
asked Siegfried, "Are you happy?" "What?" Siegfried asked
over the noise of the rakes. "Are you happy?" Kurt shouted.
It was hot and the asphalt stank. "Don't answer him," Karl
said, "He's laughing at you." "Now I'm not so happy,"
Siegfried thought, "but that's how life is. Sometimes you're
happy, sometimes you're not happy. But you're usually not
sad and not happy." Siegfried was filled with pleasure at having such serious thoughts.

"In the beginning," the melamed says, "God created—
shush, Itsikl—the heaven and the earth." Itsikl stretches a
rubber band from his chair to the table and strums it like a

1. In German: "Kraft durch Freude" - The name of the voluntary public work
brigades organized by the Nazis.

violin string. "And the earth,"—tsoom—"was without form and void"—tsoom. "And the spirit of God—sheygets her oyf"[1]—tsoom—"moved upon—gey aroys[2]—the face of the waters." Itsikl lifts his eyes from his string and looks the melamed in the face. "Was it quiet then as well?" "When?" asks the melamed. But Yingele sees what Itsikl sees. At the beginning there was a muffled sound in the darkness and an echo of drums. And suddenly the sound of a thousand strings and blue skies slowly rise from beneath the void. And when Itsikl's mother comes, the melamed says that Itsikl's head is somewhere else. And Yingele sees in his mind's eye how everyone is looking for Itsikl's head while Itsikl sits, headless, strumming "Tsoom, tsoom."

In July, Berlin stretches out for its afternoon nap. Yingele removes his shoes and places them under the stomach of the stone horse. Friedrich der Grosse sits on the horse's back with drawn sword. Then Yingele bathes his feet in the lake. The water caresses his white skin and the skullcap on his head glistens in the sun. Small ducks beat the water with their feet and hide among the water plants. In a while, Yingele thinks, the sea will part before me, and I shall be like Moses. And when the water is calm, the ducks hesitantly leave their hiding places and circle the lake. At first one duck approaches Yingele, and he is followed by others. The ducks stretch out their necks and rub their heads in Yingele's hands. But when the park guard runs up waving his stick, the ducks dive under the water and Yingele grabs his shoes from Friedrich's statue and runs for his life.

1. Yiddish - "Stop it, naughty boy."
2. Yiddish - "Get out."

In bed at night Yingele sees, in his mind's eye, Moses crossing the Red Sea with the water standing upright like a wall on
each side. The park guard runs after Moses shouting, "Heraus. Heraus."[1] But when Moses raises his arms to the heavens, the waters of the sea close in on the park guard. His head
bobs for a moment like a fisherman's cork and then sinks to
the bottom like a stone. But the ducks, thinks Yingele, will
cross over on dry land.

"Can God," Itsikl asks, "create a stone so heavy that he cannot lift it?" And Yingele can't stop thinking about this question. If he had plucked up enough courage, he would have
asked old Levin, the bookbinder. Levin's face is like the face
of God. But Yingele looks at Levin's white beard and keeps
silent. "Vus vilstu?"[2] Levin says as he picks up a book from
the table. Yingele does a mental calculation how many books
old Levin could pick up before he collapsed under their
weight. "There is no candy here," Levin says, and Yingele
remembers that Levin's wife took her own life. "She ended
her life," Joseph said, and Yingele was filled with wonder
that one could put an end to one's own life. In his mind's eye
Yingele sees Levin's wife come through the back door and
stand behind her husband. "Vus vilstu?" Levin says. "I wish
to die," Levin's wife says. "There's no candy here," says
Levin. "Just one," Levin's wife pleads. "None," Levin says,
"None."

And once Yingele found a bird in the park. Its legs fumbled
at the air and its body trembled. Yingele carried the bird in
the palm of his hand to Alexanderplatz, laid it in a box and

1. German - "Out. Out."
2. Yiddish - "What do you want?"

covered it with pieces of cloth. But in the morning its eyes were shut and its body frozen. "What a pity," Joseph said, "it is dead." And in remembering the bird, Yingele understands that God cannot lift the stone.

In August Yingele and Itsikl dig behind the shop of Solomon the butcher. Itsikl is certain there is gold treasure buried in the ground, and reveals the secret only to Yingele. When worms crawl out from the ground, Itsikl is pleased. "A sign," he says, "that the treasure is near." Itsikl will buy a violin with the gold coins they find, and promises to give the rest to Yingele. But Yingele doesn't know what to do with his share of the coins.

In September, when Joseph enters Herr Schloss's fabric shop, Hans smiles from ear to ear. Hans's mother had a difficult delivery and the doctor placed a pair of tongs on the baby's head and pulled it out. Hans's skull is therefore deformed and his mind somewhat enfeebled. But Herr Schloss turns away from Joseph and says to the empty air, "Es tut mir leid."[1] And since in normal times Herr Schloss was in the habit of greeting Joseph with pleasure, Joseph immediately understands that Herr Schloss has decided not to sell any more cloth to his kind and leaves the shop. "Dankeschön," Hans calls after him, "Dankeschön." In Auguststrasse smells of autumn fill the air. A fair-haired woman with a painted face leans against the door of a hotel. "Komm," she calls after Joseph, "Komm." And when Joseph doesn't raise his head, she whispers softly, "Kim, Kim."[2] Joseph looks at her and smiles. The woman waves her hand and smiles back. "Es tut mir leid," Joseph says. "Never mind," the woman says, "some other time."

1. German - "I am sorry."
2. Yiddish - "Come."

"One goy," Joseph says. "Never mind," the woman says, "sometime." "One goy," Joseph thinks to himself, "makes up for the wrongs of another."

But when Joseph returns home, his hands are trembling, and he cannot grip the needle. He pours himself a glass of tea, sits at the tailor's table and leafs through Yingele's book. Yingele loves to look at pictures of animals. So Joseph went to the bookshop on Potsdamstrasse and bought a book for Yingele. Yingele takes great pleasure in his book, and finds in it the fish of the oceans, and the birds of the skies, and the beasts of the fields, and everything that crawls on the face of the earth. And the book gives the German version of Genesis. Joseph reads: "The mammals appeared in the world two hundred million years ago. They are warm-blooded and covered with fur. Apart from the duckbilled platypus and the porcupine anteater, all mammals give birth to live young and the females nurse their young. The most widely distributed mammal, after man, is the mouse." Once, Joseph thinks, the mice had a king and a capital city. In His image and likeness He made them. Male and female. Now only whiskers remain, and eyes that run about in their holes. And sometimes, in the darkness, a tiny mouse is born. A picture takes shape in his mind's eye. The voice of God walks in the garden and calls out: "Mammal, Mammal, Where art thou?"

ף

BECAUSE OF THE TROUBLED TIMES YINGELE does not go out into the street or to the park anymore. When he comes back from the Hebrew classes, he puts his chin on the tailor's table and looks at his father. And although in the

eyes of the Germans Joseph's stature had dwindled, in Yingele's eyes in those days his father had grown until he
seemed like an ancient oak that provided food for all. Creatures tunnel in his trunk, lay eggs in his bark, chew his
leaves, and eat his acorns.

At night, in Yingele's dream, Joseph stands with his feet on
the ground and his head in the sky. In one hand he holds a
needle, and when his hand moves, the stars in outer space
also move. He inserts the needle in the trousers of Herr
Joachim, and the sun sets. And when he withdraws the needle with his other hand, the moon rises. He again inserts it
and the moon sets, and when he pulls it out, the sun rises.
And from among the lights in the heavens Moses comes
down from Mt. Sinai, step by step, stitch by stitch. But when
Yingele sees in his dream that the breath of life in his own
nostrils also goes in and out with the movements of Joseph's
hand, he cannot breathe properly.

When they returned to camp and lay down to rest under the
trees, Kurt Becker came and set himself next to Siegfried.
"So," he asked, "you think there's a God?" "Sure," Siegfried
said, "why do you ask?" "Because," Kurt said, "if he exists,
why don't we see him?" "Anyone who has to, sees him all
right," Siegfried said. "So," Kurt asked, "you think you'll see
him sometime?" "Are you crazy?" Siegfried said.

The soul of Heinrich Rindfleisch, professor of zoology,
yearned for a chrysalis. "I am going out to look for a
chrysalis," he said to Lieselotte and left half a potato on his
plate. Beside the almond tree, his shoes squeezed his feet,
and sweat gathered under his armpits. "If I find a chrysalis,"
he thought to himself, "my theory will be flawless." He

found one. He put it on the table in Lieselotte's kitchen inside a jam jar. In the morning Heinrich peeped inside the jar and saw a female moth. In the afternoon the cat devoured it. But in the evening many moths entered through the window and banged against the sides of the empty jar. "Aha!" Heinrich said, and wrote in his notebook:

Luna Microlepidoptera. Female: Wingspan 54 millimeters. Antennae in the form of a wire. Male: Wingspan 39 millimeters. Antennae like wires. The female Luna moth apparently emits a distinctive odor, and the male discovers her location by means of scent cells concentrated in its antennae. (I was unaware of the odor.)

In the middle of the night Heinrich went to bed. Lieselotte was there. He saw her.

And when Luna
Looked
At Heinrich
What did she see?

"It is incumbent on me," Heinrich Rindfleisch said, "to investigate how bats fly in the dark." He covered a bat's head with a black cap. When he removed the cap, he sealed the bat's nostrils with wax. The next day he extracted the bat's eyes, and on the balcony he cut off its ears. And on Tuesday afternoon he wrote down pedantically: "Bats fly even without sense organs."

Heinrich also has dreams. White forests. Line after line of letters on a copper plate. And sometimes the dreams have a tint of light blue. A kind of dim messianic note. Work and rest. Work and rest. And, at the farthest end of it all, a Great German gathers unto himself all the orderly thoughts. Perhaps everything goes on and on like a pale facsimile. Hands folded on the knees. A church organ. Anyone who disturbs stands quietly in the corner.

While Joseph and Yingele were walking down Universitäts-Strasse, a German woman placed herself in front of them and looked them up and down, and it was clear from her expression that she was satisfied by what she saw. She had, she said, been Professor Gustav Hochstraaten's secretary for many years, and if the gentleman would be so kind as to perform, for a fee of course, a service in the Wissenschaft[1] of the Professor, she would take them to him. And since Joseph's income had fallen off in those days, they followed her. When they arrived at the Professor's office the Professor said, "Pleased to meet you," and asked Joseph where he came from and when he arrived in Germany and whether Yingele was his son. And when Joseph's answers had satisfied him, he told them to follow him and walked in front of them until they came to a wide hall packed with spectators. When the Professor entered all the spectators straightened their backs. First the Professor introduced the "honored guests." Then he spoke about the differences between one Rasse[2] and another Rasse. When he had finished saying this, he took out a caliper with two arms that go up and down, placed it against Yingele's head, and called out his measurements, and everyone wrote the measurements down in their notebooks. But when he placed the caliper on Joseph's head, the lower arm got entangled in the beard, and for a moment Professor Hochstraaten's face was suffused with anger. When they re-

1. German - Science.
2. German - Race.

turned to the German woman, the Professor ordered her to pay them two marks for their trouble. And when they left, Yingele asked why the man had measured their heads, but Joseph only took out one whole mark and told Yingele to go into a bakery and buy himself whatever he fancied. And Yingele went into the shop and chose a large raisin cake.

When they got back to Alexanderplatz, Yingele went to the shop of Pomeranz, the watchmaker, and told Pomeranz what had happened. And Pomeranz said that the creed of the German requires him, on Easter, to bake a loaf of bread the size of a Jewish child's head. Pomeranz then let Yingele put the watchmaker's loupe to his eye, and Yingele looked at the intestines of a watch and saw that the wheels and springs moved in perfect harmony.

ח

AT TIMES YINGELE LONGS TO BE LIKE THE others, with straw-colored hair and pale eyes. When he sees his image in the mirror, he wants to be separated from it. From now on he thinks, and hopes that his thoughts are getting there, it will have to stand on its own. And from the expression on the face in the mirror, Yingele understands that it too is determined not to cling to him any longer. "So goodbye," Yingele says and turns to go. But out of the corner of his eye, he sees that the image has also turned to go the same way. Yingele stares at it and says, "No. You stay here and I'll go." But the image in the mirror stares back at Yingele and says exactly what he said. "All right," then Yingele thinks, "you go your way and I'll stand here." But the image in the mirror also stands and waits to see what Yingele will do. I cannot be other than I am, Yingele thinks, and is filled with sadness.

At first each team set up its own tent. Karl, Siegfried and Kurt Becker were together. Karl and Siegfried tightened the canvas and Kurt Becker hit the tent peg with the heel of his shoe. In his hands he held an imaginary mandolin and sang:

> Of all the fruit in the world
> She only wants a banana.
> Tomorrow I sail to Havana
> To bring her a banana.

"Shut up," Karl said. "Don't you like bananas?" Kurt Becker asked. Karl did not answer. "Siegfried, do you like bananas?" Kurt Becker asked Siegfried. "Yes," Siegfried said.

When they were training to fight with clubs, Kurt disappeared for a long time, and when he returned to camp he explained that he had gone to the forest to relieve himself. The leader praised Siegfried's left-handed blows. And when everyone stood up and sang, "Arise, brothers. Hear the trumpet call," Siegfried thought, "I'm happy I'm here and not somewhere else."

At night Kurt Becker whispered, "Siegfried." "What," Siegfried said. "When you unscrew your head," Kurt asked, "do you turn it to the left or to the right?" Siegfried raised his hand and felt his neck. The neck, he thought, is attached to the head like a screw. But he did not know how to answer Kurt. It's too bad, he thought, that Karl is asleep. He would have already told Kurt the right answer. Siegfried lay for a long time gaping at the canvas ceiling and racking his brains. Finally he said, "Kiss my ass."

On the first day of the week, which the Germans call Sonntag, a group of Germans walks towards Yingele. As Yingele draws near, they block his path and ask, "Where to?" "To shul," Yingele says. "In your schule," the Germans say, "there must be plenty of nails." "I don't know if there are any," Yingele says. "There are," the Germans say. "Maybe there are," Yingele says. "Sure there are," the Germans say, "because otherwise, how could you nail God's body to the Cross?"

And Yingele remembers that once he saw a picture of the Holy Family. In the middle a woman sat with a baby in her lap. Blue eyes. Somewhat fat. A yellow light arose from the woman. A yellow light arose from the baby in her lap. Others stood there; one in a nightgown and another with a muslin cap. All of them looked at the sky below the top of the frame. But in the corner sat an old man with a bent back. He was fixing some kind of box or cupboard. You cannot fix a cupboard, Yingele thought, if you don't look at it.

"How?" one of the Germans says and puts his nose in Yingele's face. "I didn't do it," Yingele assures him. "Yes you did," the Germans say. "I didn't do it," Yingele says. "Yes you did," they say and push him against the wall. The picture of *my* family, Yingele thinks, is brown. Joseph is wearing a suit and a hat on his head, and I'm wearing my white shirt. There was a paper knight in Klein's photography shop, and Yingele wanted to put his head through the round hole above its neck, but Joseph was in a hurry to return to his workshop because of Schultz's suit that "must be finished."

Even though Yingele is terrified, he is determined not to admit having done anything. And when the Germans see that Yingele's resolve is firm, they decide to leave him alone. But one of them grabs hold of his coat collar and demands that he

swear not to commit the offense again. Yingele swears. And
when they leave him alone, Yingele does not go on to the
shul, but returns to his house on Alexanderplatz. After
telling Joseph what happened, he bursts out crying. He does
not cry because of the things the Germans said, but rather
because of the vow he made. And Joseph folds his palms together and sticks out a finger and thumb and shows Yingele
that the shadow on the wall has the shape of a bird.

But when Yingele goes to sleep, Joseph remembers what
happened and his head spins. Someone, Joseph thinks, enters a tavern, and someone goes by in the street, and a
woman looks in the mirror, and a dog sniffs another dog's
rear, and a fly buzzes on the window pane, and grass in the
field, and someone lays tefillin,[1] and another kneels, a mole
in its hole, stars in the sky, cakes, diamonds and vineyards,
babies and ink, someone marches from right to left, and another says "blue," and tomatoes and fish in the water and a
rainbow in the clouds and kings and prophets and lentil soup
and verses from the prayer book and nightgowns and blood
and sighs and the ringing of bells and meatballs and fingernails . . . and he grasps his ruler and forces himself to
think: "thirty-six above, fifty-eight below."

"The world of forms," Pomeranz says, "is insubstantial and
nothing but the reflection of another world which contains
no forms at all." And it seems to Yingele too that the images
that come his way—the kitchen clock whose hands always
show eight-thirty, and the sign "Industrial Bank" above the
marble building, and a black poodle, and a woman with a
sunbonnet, and the moss on the wall in Alexanderplatz—

_____
1. Hebrew - phylacteries.

are not real images, but only pictures that go in and out of the mirror. If only, Yingele thinks, I could see the hidden side of the mirror. And he closes his eyes like the old man in the park and waits for another image to form in his mind. In his imagination Yingele sees Pomeranz walking to the end of the world. And when he passes the last form, he takes out his watchmaker's loupe and says, "At last." Pomeranz's body then floats in empty space.

ט

A YELLOW DOG WHOSE FRONT FOOT HAS been amputated sniffs the corners of the houses on Alexanderplatz. When it sees Solomon, the butcher, it barks at him in fury and Solomon mutters, "Gey avek,"[1] but the dog bares its teeth until Solomon disappears behind his shop door. "It's because he's full of blood," Fride says. The dog now lies down next to the drunken German on the corner of Friedrichstrasse, and puts its head on his knees. The drunk looks at Yingele who is looking at the dog, and says, "Give me five pfenning and I'll tell you where the Good Lord is." Yingele searches his pockets and finds three pfenning and hands them over to the drunk. The drunk motions to Yingele to bend his head and put his ear near his mouth and then whispers, "In the bottom of the bottle." And when he sees Yingele standing and looking at him and not going away, he asks for another three pfenning in exchange for which he'll teach Yingele a song. And when Yingele says he has nothing left in his pockets, the drunk says that the song is also about nothing, and so he will teach it to him for nothing:

1. Yiddish - "Go away from here."

Ick sitze da
Und esse klops
Uff eemal klopts
Ick denk: Na nu?
Na nu? denk ick
Ick geh heraus und kieke
Und wer steht draussen?
Icke[1]

And Yingele immediately realizes that this is not just any old song and silently thanks the drunk for teaching him for free a song worth at least ten marks. All week Yingele thinks about the song, but he understands it only on the Sabbath when he sees the cat chasing its own shadow.

Kurt Becker's pocketknife has five blades, a bottle opener and a screwdriver. Its exterior is overlaid with ivory and on the surface there is an eagle with outstretched wings. Siegfried saw a pocketknife like that in a store, but it was even more expensive than an axe. At times Siegfried sees, in a kind of wonderful fantasy, a dwarf who sneaks into his room at night and puts a pocketknife like that on the chair next to his bed. Then he walks up and down Friedrichstrasse, pulling out the blades one by one and replacing them, and everyone looks. And when the teacher said, "The Middle Ages were a period of darkness in human history which came to an end with the Renaissance," it seemed to Siegfried that this time he understood what she had said. And on the last day, as everyone was folding up the tents, Siegfried took his father's old razor out of his pocket and cut the straps of Kurt Becker's knapsack.

1. Yiddish - I'm sitting there/ Eating meatballs./ A sudden knock./ I think: who's there?/ Who's there? I think/ I go and look/ Who's standing there?/ Me

When the edicts increased in frequency, the Jews fled wherever they could. The Poles amongst them were taken by the
Germans, who threw them over the wall that stands between
Germany and Poland so that they would get up and go back
whence they came. And in his mind's eye Joseph sees
Kamashenmakher, the matchmaker, and old Levin, the
bookbinder, shake off the mud that had stuck to their clothes
from the fall; and they go back to the town which they left for
Germany. And the Poles welcome them with open arms and
say, "Blessed be the Good Lord! Thirty years! Our lives were
not worth living." "Go to the Dutch," Pomeranz says to
Joseph, "and they will give you a paper, and you will be able
to settle in their country." This being the case, Joseph went
to the house of the Dutch ambassador in Berlin. But when he
saw that on the wall of the house was written, among other
things, Kantoor,[1] he returned to Alexanderplatz. Then an
order was issued that all the Jews must present their papers
before the authorities. The German took Joseph's papers and
wrote something.[2] And when Joseph left, he glanced at the
paper and saw that the German had written "Israel" next to
his name, and a kind of joy crept into his heart.

But in Joseph's sleep, a distant picture rises like a bubble
from a sinking ship. A man is going down wooden stairs.
Moonlight falls on his nightgown, but his face is wrapped in
darkness. The man always goes down and never comes up.
Sometimes Joseph thinks the man is Uncle Pinye whose
spirit had dimmed and who shut himself up in the attic until
he died; and sometimes it seems to him that the man is
Joseph himself. "Dreams," Pomeranz the watchmaker says,

1. Dutch - Office.
2. In 1938 all Jewish males were obliged to add "Israel" to their name, and all
Jewish females "Sarah."

"signify nothing." But Joseph thinks a man's nights are a mirror of his days, because at night man doubles himself like his reflection in the mirror, and in that same reflection is hidden the secret of his existence. "But," Joseph says, "a man looks at the reflection and doesn't understand the secret." "A man," Pomeranz says, "is like a clock whose face tells the time because of the wheels and springs that move inside his brain." "A clock," Joseph says, "cannot read the time on its face, but man sometimes knows where he came from and where he is going." "Where from, Joseph, and where to?" Pomeranz sighs. And Joseph gets up from his chair and pours tea and cuts two slices of lemon as thin as paper. And Pomeranz sips the tea, and his forehead is covered with sweat, and he takes off his glasses and cleans them on his shirttail. "One must escape while there is still time, Joseph," Pomeranz says.

And Joseph remembers that before his Bar Mitzvah he traveled with his father, Reb Chaim, to see the Rabbi of Kishinev in person. And on the train he looked at the face of an old Russian woman and saw that the fields outside were passing by inside her eyes. At first he did not know where those same fields went to from there, but when he looked at the face of another Russian, he saw they were inside his eyes. In the morning Reb Chaim stood in the corridor and laid tefillin. The old woman's eyes were closed, but her rooster stuck its head out of the sack and looked at Joseph. Then some hooligans came by and pulled Reb Chaim's coat tails, but Reb Chaim moved his body in the morning prayer and did not look round. And when the hooligans pushed Reb Chaim, and his head hit the window glass, the rooster looked there and Joseph saw that the rooster looks at one place and then at another, but it does not look at the space between. And when the hooligans said vulgar things, the old woman woke up and sent them away in a hoarse voice, and once again the fields passed by inside her eyes. When the old woman saw that Joseph was looking at her, she took an apple out of the sack and put it on his knees. And when Reb Chaim had finished the morning prayer, he placed Joseph on his knees and both of them looked at the forests. "Sometimes," Reb Chaim said, "man needs a broken heart." It was then that Joseph saw that in Reb Chaim's eyes, too, there was a landscape, but this landscape had no form at all.

"The goy," Joseph says to Pomeranz, "is cruel everywhere." And he lays the measuring tape on the cloth and draws a white chalk line and picks up the scissors and cuts the cloth along the line. And in so doing, Joseph also splits in two, and one half of him speaks to the other. "What does all this mean?" the first half asks. "Oh, no. You tell me," the second half answers. "My days," the first half says, "are like a declining shadow." "And I," the second half says, "am like withered grass." But when Yingele comes in and leans his chin on the tailor's table, Joseph's two halves again become one.

᠊᠎᠎᠎᠎᠎᠎

THE KING OF THE VIKINGS IN THE CARTOON strips is cruel to his enemies but generous to those who are loyal to him. This week the king of the Vikings pressed General Olaf to his heart and said, "Olaf, my son, it is only because of your courage that we have won this battle." In the surrounding fields were strewn the bodies of the enemy. I am already eighteen years old, Siegfried thought. He put on his coat and went out to Friedrichstrasse. The trams were not running because of the heavy snow. Only wayfarers passed by from time to time, keeping close to the walls of the houses. Grey skies stood above the roofs. Siegfried packed a snowball in his palm and threw it at the street lamp. The snow clung to the surface of the glass and clumps dropped off on to the pavement. On the other side of the street, a man in a long overcoat was walking in the direction of Alexander-platz. Siegfried picked up a piece of brick and pressed snow around it. As the snowball flew over the tram tracks, the snow fell off but the brick continued on its flight and hit the man in the back. The man groaned and looked up. When he saw Siegfried he hesitated for a moment and then crossed the street, his cane groping its way through the snow. But when he stood before Siegfried and looked in his face, he only moved his lips and said nothing. He turned around and headed towards Alexanderplatz.

They found Miriam in a cradle on the paving stones of Alexanderplatz. And since she ceased crying when Pomer-anz the watchmaker held her in his arms, Pomeranz took her home. And even though he could never fathom her, Pomer-anz loved Miriam with his whole heart and his wife Gitl raised her as though she were her own flesh and blood. At first Miriam was called by another name, but when she was five she insisted they call her Miriam. Gitl pleaded with her not to talk such nonsense, but Pomeranz resigned himself to the name and said nothing.

When the shop is empty, Pomeranz reads Spinoza's book. "We should derive everything," thinks Pomeranz, "in accor-dance with the light of reason." Sometimes he ponders on things until causes and effects cleave to one another like exquisite clockwork, and he almost sees how everything fits together through the power of reason.

> And how does
> Spinoza
> Explain
> Gitl's slippers?

Pomeranz wishes to understand the purpose of things, while Miriam sees their form, and the difference between himself and Miriam fills his heart with foreboding and he does not know if this fear is for Miriam or himself. He piles pillows on the chair, seats her down, puts the watchmaker's loupe to her eye and Miriam looks at the interior of a watch for a long time. Pomeranz wants to teach her how the spring is wound up and how because of this, a wheel turns and this wheel turns its neighbor, and so on. But Miriam does not listen at all. In the evening Miriam draws springs and wheels with marvelous accuracy; but they are all disconnected and do not touch each other at all. And when Pomeranz picks up a pencil and adds the face of a clock in the corner of the paper, Miriam bursts into tears and says, "Now it's all ruined."

Sometimes it seems to Pomeranz that Miriam sees straight to the heart of the matter, and does not need the steps of reason. But this kind of vision, Pomeranz thinks, is a mixed blessing. Indeed, when a man sees things straight, he may arrive at once where others can come only by roundabout means. But when you lack such vision, you fall, God forbid, into an abyss. And that is why Pomeranz's heart is filled with horror.

Once a man entered the watchmaker's shop and asked the price of a gold watch. He had already made up his mind to buy the watch, but Miriam looked at him with angry eyes and told him to go away, and the man was filled with such rage that he dropped the watch and left. And at the tanner's apprentice, who is feeble-minded and comes in only to ask the time, Miriam smiles with affection and puts her hand in his.

The Song of Solomon
And His Golden Watch

Take it, Lily,
Don't be silly.
Thy cheeks are comely
With rows of jewels.
Don't be silly,
Take it, Lily.
Thy neck
With chains of gold.

"I shall shortly die," Miriam says. Her body is the age of nineteen and is completely healthy, but there is a strange spirit within. In most people, Joseph thinks, lives the soul of a dog that looks through the holes of its eyes in submission and only wishes to please its master; but in Miriam's body lives the soul of a cat that contracts its pupils, removes the picture of the world and remains sealed like a mountain.

Gitl is sure that Miriam's mind will settle down when she gets married, and Pomeranz pretends to agree with her, but when he tries to draw a mental picture of Miriam as a man's wife, he cannot do so. "What can I do?" he says to Joseph, "she doesn't want to be married off." Fride the insane, Joseph thinks, and Herr Wermus and the chickens in

Solomon's shop have skin as hard and rough as a sack. And inside that sack there is flesh and bones and blood. But Miriam, he thinks, is like those butterflies that come to the park in the summer, and powder falls off their bodies and they become as transparent as glass. Joseph sees himself, in his mind's eye, cutting Miriam's flesh and there is no blood. And he remembers a story he once heard about a daughter of the gods who came down from the heavens and mated with a human and that is why the foundations of the world were undermined and the seasons became entangled. "Her soul," Joseph says, "is pure." And he does not say, "as the souls of the beasts of the fields," in order not to frighten Pomeranz.

When Miriam stands with Joseph and Yingele in the zoo, the leopard looks at Joseph with Miriam's eyes. When all the animals entered the ark, Joseph thinks to himself, the leopard remained alone, like a cliff, age upon age, until the waters receded. And when the world was renewed, only the leopard remembered that once birds had flown in the depths of the ocean and fish had swum in the skies. And since he understands the leopard's secret, Joseph's soul is transposed and the leopard looks at Miriam with Joseph's eyes. And at that moment Joseph does not know if he will still have the strength to hold a needle. Trousers, Herr Schultz? And what did you wear before your mother was born? But when Miriam laughs at the monkeys' pranks, Joseph understands that she dwells in both worlds at the same time.

> He will hang his coat
> On a sunbeam.

He will capture the music
Of her gown.
Her children will become
The wind.
His shadow will embrace her and
Fall down.

Miriam rolls her dress up to her thighs, her soul as naked as
a fish, and wades in the river Spree. Miriam is not ashamed
of her body. And the river that flows to the sea and is never
full hides in the shadow of its bridge and caresses her legs.
And Yingele's hand is in Miriam's hand, and he is nothing but another Miriam-body, a duplicate of her own. Oh
Berlin, Joseph thinks, how privileged are thy waters.

When Karl's parents moved to Munich, Karl gave Siegfried
his German shepherd dog as a present. Siegfried first banged
nails into the old storeroom in the yard, and then put the dog
inside. "Kaiser, komm her," Siegfried said. But Kaiser only
looked at Siegfried with his black eyes and did not move.
"Kaiser, komm her," Siegfried said again. Kaiser blinked his
eyes and lowered his ears. "Kaiser, komm her," Siegfried
said for the third time. Kaiser wiggled his tail but did not
budge.

When Miriam is near him, Joseph's body is fit to break.
Miriam is transparent as the air, and though she knows
nothing, her eyes take in everything. A woman and yet not a
woman, she is nevertheless a woman. And how, Joseph
thinks, shall I enter that shrine? When Adam knew Eve the
snake was already inside her body, but Miriam has come into
the world before being born. When she is born, Joseph

thinks, she will die. Joseph hopes to find some flaw in Miriam so that she will be saved. And that's why he says deliberately, "Today I walked past the Reichstag." "Today?" Miriam asks. "Today," Joseph says and repeats, "past the Reichstag." "This coat—who is it for?" Miriam asks. "A judge," Joseph says and purposely adds, "and his name is Herr Hohenzoller." "A strange color," Miriam says. "He is a strange man," Joseph says. "Joseph is also a strange man," Miriam says, "Why doesn't he calm down?"

Afterwards Miriam is immersed in thought and bites her fingernails. Joseph looks at her fingers and compels himself to think that they are just like all fingers. But Joseph's heart yearns for Miriam's hands, and he clenches his fist until the nails pierce his flesh. Miriam asks for a glass of water. And while she is drinking from the glass, Joseph looks at her mouth through the water which he sees through the glass and thinks, "Water will join with water."

And suddenly the fever in Joseph's body abates, and he is a very old man whose bones are hollow like a bird's. Now Joseph remembers all the changes of seasons since the creation of the world. And from that far distance, he can look straight at Miriam and talk about trifles.

"I shall be a cat," Yingele says. "I shall be a mouse," Miriam says. And Yingele chases after her and grabs hold of her legs. She bends over Yingele's body and bites his shoulder. He does not ask her to let go of him, but bites her leg hard. Miriam's teeth are in his flesh, and the salty taste of her flesh is on his tongue. He lets up a bit and so does she. He bites gently and Miriam bites back. Yingele now forgets that he is

a cat and imagines his body being devoured limb by limb
until all of it is in her stomach.

Yingele is a kind of holy
Child who does not need
A womb.
He is asleep on the wooden floor
In Alexanderplatz and next to him
Miriam. She did not bear
Him, but Joseph
Loves her. In a strange way
He is also hers. The seed
Which Joseph planted inside Chaya-Leah emerges
From the body of Miriam
An ancient story that was forecast by
Astrologers one thousand
Nine hundred years ago. And what say
The astrologers who walk
The streets of Berlin?
A child
Who was created from the seed of man without a
    woman's womb
Will rise
To the heavens
Next
Year
And he will take with him
And he will take with him
All our sins
All our sins
And in exchange for the effort made
(But first he must trim his fingernails)
He will be God for about

Three thousand years.
And his mother who did not bear
Him will become a saint
And his father will be (with a percentage of the take)
Patron of the tailors

"I shall come at night, Joseph," Miriam says. "Bitterly," Joseph thinks, "she weeps in the night, her cheeks wet with tears." His hand is extended and the needle shines. Now he inserts the needle. "I am sewing the skin of my body," Joseph thinks and pulls the needle out the other side of the cloth. "Don't you want me, Joseph?" Miriam asks, and Joseph looks into her eyes and sees they are transparent as crystal, and he longs for her body the way he longs for the body of Yingele. I will put her thin fingers, Joseph thinks, whose nails are bitten down, into my mouth one by one. But Joseph knows that such an hour belongs to another world, and man should not confound the worlds lest he go mad. "Thy two breasts," Joseph thinks, "are like two young roes that are twins," and he pictures to himself how he will caress Miriam's breasts until her nipples harden. Ten thousand years of exile, Joseph thinks, and at their end, redemption. And when Yingele comes in Miriam grasps his waist and laughs, "I'll come to *you* tonight, all right?" "All right," Yingele says.

All his life Siegfried Stopf never doubted that he was Siegfried Stopf. Whenever he heard his name he always answered without hesitation, "Yah." Only Still, the tobacco-seller on Friedrichstrasse, saw what he saw and his heart filled with dread. And when Siegfried placed a pfennig coin on the counter and said "Zwo,"[1] Herr Still put two cigarettes

1. German dialect - "Two."

before him but looked away. "This disaster," Herr Still thought, "must have its origins at the dawn of history."

From the day Miriam said what she said, the door to the house remained open. "When she comes," Joseph thinks, "when she comes . . ." His thoughts are not articulated anymore. He keeps on sewing. "Orange blossom," Joseph thinks. Here I sit, Joseph thinks, and sew and think about orange blossom. Why, Joseph thinks, do I think about orange blossom? Is orange blossom golden? Gold flowers, Joseph thinks, are not flowers at all. Orange blossom is white. And in his mind's eye Joseph sees a tree of gold speckled with white flowers. And he saws the tree from the trunk upwards, stitch after stitch. The clock strikes midnight.

At dawn Yingele cries in his sleep and Joseph carries his body to his own bed. "Take now thy son," Joseph thinks, "thine only son," he thinks, "whom thou lovest." Yingele tucks his legs into Joseph's stomach and calms down. The skies of Berlin are already bright behind the curtain.

Herr Still, the tobacco-seller on Friedrichstrasse, once plucked up his courage and spoke to Siegfried. "I came from Austria," Herr Still said. "Na, Yah," Siegfried said. "From a village called Heiligenblut,"[1] Herr Still said. "Na, Yah," Siegfried said. "That village," Herr Still said, "is near the Crossglöckner."[2] Siegfried said nothing. "The mountains there," Herr Still said, "reflect the thunder, which reverberates in the valley like a giant bell." "Na, Yah," Siegfried said. Herr Still felt the dread spreading in his chest. "What would

1. German - Holy Blood (a village in Austria).
2. German - The Great Bellringer (a mountain range in Austria).

you like?" he asked. "Zwo," Siegfried said and laid the pfennig on the counter.

אי

JOSEPH IS A SATYR-BUTTERFLY. HIS BODY IS
brown velvet. He hovers to and fro in search of Miriam.
Here are her outstretched wings, a nymph-butterfly. Four
powdery eyes on her wings. Nuptial flight. Flowers also fly.
Space is anointed with color. She stretches her antennae out
to him. He stretches his wings. Her body quivers. Lightning
flashes in his eyes.

Joseph is a seahorse. With an armored body. His fringes
quiver in the water. Among the seaweed is a female seahorse.
She twitches her tail. He bends his head. They straighten
their bodies. They touch and part. Their skin shines in a
blaze of color. A nuptial swim. Starfish also swim. Coral
cathedrals glisten orange-red. Her belly touches the seabed.
She consents. She disappears into the darkness of the depths.
She reappears. Carrying an egg. She approaches him. His
stomach is spread out. Now the egg is in his pocket of life.
His blood vessels embrace his fetus-son. Who is still transparent. His form reaches completion. His heart beats
through his skin.

Already, Herr Still thinks, the Basilisk strides the streets of
Berlin. It has the body of a rooster with the head of a snake,
and it kills with a glance. The Basilisk appears on the corner
of Friedrichstrasse at twilight to the laughing call of the
Kakabura bird. First one and then another, and finally they
all burst into song: "Hepp! Hepp! Here is our new savior!

Hepp! Hepp!" And behind the Basilisk crawls the holy iguana. Drops of blood drip from its eyes and it recites a prayer: "Spiritus sancti! Spiritus sancti! How beautiful the hour! How beautiful!"

The stone fish lies on the ocean bed like a stone covered with seaweed. The leaf fish has the shape of a fallen leaf. The gazelle thrusts its antlers into the foliage and freezes in place. And the owl, whose eyes are fixed in their sockets, turns its head. Only the salmon returns to the river it remembers. And there is an ancient fable: The Basilisk will die if it looks at its own reflection in the mirror. But alas! The Basilisk is in love with its face. It is pulling a comb through its hair.

Nineteen hundred and thirty-eight. November the ninth.

Joseph Silverman sews. A Psalm of David. The Lord is my shepherd, I shall not want. He maketh me to lie down in green pastures. He leadeth me, he sews, beside the still waters. He restoreth my soul, he sews, He leadeth me in the paths of righteousness for His name's sake.

The paths of two yellow-haired, blue-eyed gods cross in a celestial lane. "Guten Tag." "Guten Tag." One is somewhat bald, and the other has a large paunch. "Wohin denn?"[1] "Arbeit,[2] Arbeit." Today we have to spread fine crystal glass over Bayern, Rheinus, Sauerland, Hünsruck, Schwarzwald and so on, and our little copycats in Pilsen and in Dresden, in Schtetin and in Hamburg are emerging, skull by skull, in Frankfurt and Mannhein and in Berlin and in Hanover, and skull by skull in Munchen, too.

1. German - "Where to?"
2. German - "Work."

Joseph Silverman sews. Yea, though I walk through the valley of the shadow of death, I will fear no evil, for thou art, he sews, with me. Thy rod and thy staff, he sews, they comfort me.

"Straighten it a little here." "Straighten it a little there." Right on time. A sky properly made of fine crystal glass now divides the ancient heavens from the Vaterland.[1] And meanwhile, until sunrise, sauerkraut star dust, celestial sausages, and a glass of beer from the galactic barrel. "Prosit!"[2]

Joseph Silverman sews. Thou preparest a table before me, he sews, in the presence of mine enemies. Thou anointest my head with oil, he sews, my cup runneth over.

Success. The crystal reddens. Especially that part over Berlin. Look. Dresden and Munchen are also visible. Oh, what a feast! Only fair-haired gods have such aesthetics. Fireworks and smoke, glass, and human voices. This is now the first part of the symphony. What harmony!

Joseph Silverman sews, surely goodness and mercy, he sews, shall follow me all the days of my life. And I will dwell in the house of the Lord, he sews, forever. . . .

Siegfried raised the club and hit Yingele's head, a single blow. From the force of that blow, Yingele's skull caved in and a bone splinter like a knife split Yingele's brain in that place where the dreams reside. And when Joseph saw the blood from Yingele's head streaming down his face, his heart broke.

1. German - The fatherland.
2. German - "Drink up."

As for the rest, it is already written in the history books that Joseph was left up there, alone, and said, "Mayn got, mayn got, farvos hastu mikh farlozn!"[1] and died.

Siegfried raised the club for the second time and hit Joseph on the chest, a single blow. And from the force of that blow, Joseph's heart of flesh also split. "Na," Siegfried thought, "I'm already quite good with a club."

י'

AND AFTER THE CONFLAGRATION, GERMANY remained as transparent as crystal. Everywhere they said "Please" and "Thank you" with the proper accent. Only acceptable odors floated in the air. No one strayed from the subject of conversation. Jokes were rationed and told in stages.

Silence reigned in Alexanderplatz. Four slaughtered chickens looked out from Solomon's shop with inverted eyes. But since they had died by Kosher slaughter, there was no one to take them off the hook. Only the German drunkard from the corner of Friedrichstrasse wandered about Alexanderplatz, and the yellow dog whose front leg was cut off limped after him. "Even though I didn't drink more than usual today . . . ," the drunkard thought (what the dog thought we shall never know). And as the day drew to a close, the drunkard sat himself down on a bench and sighed, "Where is everyone?" he said. "Where the hell is everyone?"

Suddenly he realized that all the sights he sought would never return to Alexanderplatz, and was horrified. "What

1. Yiddish - "My God, My God, why hast thou forsaken me?"

will I do?" he thought. "What will I do now?" And when the
horror passed, he was seized with longing and his heart filled
with sadness. And when his sadness soared aloft to the upper
worlds, the residents there were shaken. "Incredible!" they
called to each other, "Incredible! A German's sorrow?!" And
although that sorrow gave off the smell of wine, it was nevertheless real sorrow. So the light returned from the far west
and briefly glowed; and for a short time the dead came back
to gladden the drunkard's heart and they were, for the last
time, for him alone, what they had been while they lived.

They push the sun as it passes over
Alexanderplatz. Someone sells cheap soap.
A child cries; they took something
from him. People pretend the merchandise
is flawed. When the fan makes a noise,
they drip butter into it. A car got stuck
in the snow. In the evening the women
cry out "kim esn."[1] Someone pushes a cart.
A barber raises his knife. When his eyes
are closed he remembers his first wife.
People think. The old man on the second floor
will soon die. Children break through the gate.
When his wife screams he imagines a lion
is savaging her. The bath attendant limps.
She smells the mushrooms that he bought.
A poor man gives alms to another
poor man. The soup pots of Berlin
are heavy. "The clouds," the Rabbi thinks,
"are heading south." White mist rises
from the policeman's mouth. Someone loves
the summer. He says "Mein Herr" and smiles

1. Yiddish - "Come and eat."

to himself. The groom is a Yeshiva student
from Lithuania. It is written on the wall
"Hans's mother is a whore." The smell of soup
at the hour of prayer. "Only revolution,"
says a skinny youth. The rabbi's wife feels
the bodies of dead chickens. What does the widow
do at night? In the tanner's skins you can recognize
the animal's form. The sign of the watchmaker's shop
fell down the night of the storm.
She who used to be a singer sings
in the kitchen. The greengrocer's has been shut
for two weeks. Sometimes a man enters
the sewing shop. The middleman complains that
    everything
is getting worse. Three ugly daughters
in the family. The neighbors come in
to see the new stove. When the old woman
sits on the bench, her feet do not reach
the ground. The Messiah will come from
the direction of Friedrichstrasse. A child cries;
his mother wiped his nose too hard.
An empty cognac bottle in the synagogue yard.
Someone comes out from under the bridge
and yawns. The rich live at the end
of the street. When she cooks noodles
she remembers a river in Poland. The deaf person
sees only the movement of the sneeze. The Talmud
was signed and sealed in Alexanderplatz.
"Do you know how much this costs?"
The smell of salt fish rises from the mouth
of the melamed. Belief in God.
The dogs in Alexanderplatz are used
to the electric tram. She put flowers

in the jar where she kept the jam.
In the evening the butcher locks his shop
and counts money. The milkman's face looks
like the face of a horse. He talked about
the mole in his garden from Purim[1] to Passover.
On the Day of Atonement the fur seller's stomach
made a noise. On the bureau stands a picture
of the family. They say that the beggar
is very rich. The prophet Isaiah walks towards
Bismarckstrasse. A German draws his family tree.
When she waters the flowerpots you can see
the flesh of her arms. The bagel seller recites
verses from the psalms. In her face you can see
the face of her mother. Who got off
the last tram? The old people in the basement
once had children. Sometimes a man without a head
wanders Alexanderplatz. On the Sabbath
shouts are heard from the grocer's house.
What is down there under the ground?
He dreams about her because she had
three husbands. When the mohel[2] shakes hands,
his fingers feel soft. Horses sometimes die.
When she cries she does not lie.
Marks pass from hand to hand even
in September. A messenger boy peeks
at a pornographic magazine. They say that
her brother is a Marxist. Women are especially
beautiful on New Year. He takes medicine
on credit. When snow falls one cannot tell
the difference between Germans and Jews.

1. A Jewish holiday.
2. Circumciser.

In winter the prayers are warmer. The fur seller
moved to a different neighborhood. A woman
of about thirty with a rooster on her hip.
Alexanderplatz is a ship. A child wears
his father's trousers that she has shortened.
She holds onto the rail with both her hands.
In the wine shop everything is imprisoned
in bottles. The Rabbi's daughter boarded the tram.
The faces drawn by the street artist
are and are not a good likeness. A talisman
she received from a tsadik[1] hangs between
her breasts. A descendant of Moses pretends
he is a German. "Others have all the luck,"
she thinks as she airs the bed. When
he took in the milk the street was white.
People brood over business matters during the night.
No one listens to his war stories. A well-built youth
looks at a porcelain cup. She sewed a cloth patch
on the umbrella. A letter has been peeking
out of the mailbox for a week. The children
from the orphanage especially admire the lion.
A ninety-year-old man lives on the second floor.
Someone laughs during the prayers. The cat
cleans its ears next to the stationery shop.
When in the bath he thinks, "If only
I didn't have a wife." A thin youth
writes about life. The matchmaker praises
the furniture. During the kol nidre[2] he calculates
her age. A live chicken stares
at the dead chickens. The doctor also

1. Hasidic Rabbi.
2. The opening prayer of the Day of Atonement.

undresses at night. On weekdays only old people
come to the synagogue. They discuss the price
of furniture on a starry night. They say
she has a German lover. Someone collapsed
in the street and died. The tax collector returned
to his ill-tempered spouse. Ivy on the wall
of the money-lender's house. After the Passover meal
he felt a pain in his stomach. A child
looks for storks on the hospital roof.
The whale threw up Jonah in Alexanderplatz.
At night he looks for the medicine
in all the drawers. A mother admonishes her children
not to go far. Sometimes the shoemaker remembers
the face of a Polish soldier. Deaf and dumb people
play chess. When the rabbi opened the Aron Hako-
    desh[1]
flies flew in. On the bookbinder's table stands
a charity tin. He makes water during the slikhes.[2]
After the ritual bath her voice is soft.
What would happen if it weren't for the prayers?
The ball rolled into the fish shop.
"Aren't you from Warsaw?" he asks everyone.
The Lithuanian took his neighbor to court.
The child does not recognize his father from a
childhood picture. The drunk sees the setting of the
    moon.
In the hardware store hangs a spoon.
He says, "I'll explain it to you,"
and never does. The butcher's daughter is married
to a grocer. His thin legs jump when
the doctor taps them with a hammer.

1. Where the Holy Scriptures are kept in the synagogue.
2. Penitential prayers.

The same man always stands next to the bookshop.
The chandelier seller yawns on Sunday. His hands
in the picture are not like his hands today.
The upholsterer's cross-eyed son is a law student.
The two Shakespearean gravediggers stand
in the square. Once a German whore stood there.
The melamed's cat is especially clever. A child
whose father left beats a tin drum.
The bride and groom do not agree
on the color of the sofa. On Friday
the cantor drinks three fresh eggs. Someone
examines a coin in the moonlight. One asks
forgiveness on the high holy days. When the grocer
takes money, he has fingers like a piano player.
The midwife died. Children cross the street
as if there were something on the other side.
The moon comes especially to Alexanderplatz.
The melamed loves pickled cucumbers. Why
doesn't the sky fall? They say she wrote
poems in Poland. He resembles her brother
who stayed behind in Lublin. On Passover
Elijah will come to Alexanderplatz. A kite
got entangled in the telegraph wires. Even money
looks like flowers in her hands. The wood handle
of the Holy Scroll has split. On the way home
the rabbi lies a bit. A one-legged man
reads palms. There are two schools of thought
as to the widow's age. On the Sabbath
they talk a little less about death. Behind
the bridal veil there is an ugly face.
He remembers his teeth and returns the apple
to the box. The old dog rules over
the restaurant's garbage. In the evening

the eyes of the Germans turn green.
He holds onto his violin as if there were
a baby in the case. The Galician pays his debts
with a sour face. The gramophone handle
broke. When a German blows his nose
the sound stays in the street. There are
boring chapters in the Bible. The melamed
walks and the children walk behind.
A snowman stands near the bookshop. Debts
are paid at the end of the month. "Is there,"
he asks, "a toy for ten pfennig?"
Why do the blinds of the widow's house stand out?
Someone asks, "What's the time?" A poet
prepares a list of rhymes. Even during
the argument ants move in a single file.
When the baker's wife is asleep, she has
an innocent face. The dog gnaws the bones
from the book of Ezekiel. The Chevre Kadishe.[1]
Who cast the church bell? She kept
the fine tea until it gathered mold.
He goes to the bank only for the secretary's
fingernails. A postman passes by through
the window frame. The infant does not yet
know its name. Even when the teller is not
in the bank, he says, "At your service."
The shames[2] is dead. The doctor listens
to the widow's breathing. They have a long-
standing feud over a seat in the synagogue.
A cheap guest house. Walking backwards.
Women end their conversation and begin again.
His eyebrows were singed in the war.

1. The Jewish funeral society.
2. The caretaker of the synagogue.

She moved to Hamburg, but her name remained
on the door. The middleman pauses for a moment
to organize his lies. One eye is blind
but the coat is new. The merchant says it's not
worth it. He thinks about precisely what he wants
to forget. Orphans walk hand in hand
with greedy faces. A tin plate lay in the street
for three days. His forefathers in the picture
look at him in amazement. She hands out
to the neighbors what is left of the cake.
The fish in the shop swim as if the tub
were a lake. She knits a vest for her husband.
At night one mosquito becomes Ashmedai.[1]
The longer the prayer service, the more he hates
his father. After the Sabbath meal he picks
his teeth. He looks at her dress and thinks
about her nipples. The cake-seller's face
is like the face of a carp. Women talk
about other women. "I have to whitewash that wall,"
he has been thinking for twenty years.
The butcher's chickens sleep at night. Everyone
goes out to see the fight. "He has two houses,"
the matchmaker whispers to the widow. A retired
teacher breaks wind. When he takes off his glasses,
he looks at nothing. The land of Jesus
is behind the "Industrial Bank." One shoulder
is lower than the other. At night he puts
his teeth in a glass. In summer
the trams pass through the houses. The barber
stands at the entrance of his shop and picks
his nose. The midwife's legs have swollen veins.

---

1. Prince of the demons.

The Germans seem far away when it rains.
The cantor opens an umbrella. Once a whore
entered the houseware shop. From her face
it is clear that she will reprimand
her daughter after the prayers. A coffin
passes through a nearby street. When he crosses
the bridge, he remembers that he was a child.
An egg yolk stain on Heine's book of poems.
The widow's laundry. There is a bottle cap
and sewing thread in the boy's pocket.
When she says, "Oy Vey," he remembers
his mother. The dead greet one another.
There is a black tooth in the doctor's face.
When one enters a house one kisses
the Mezzuza.[1] The shoe store lacks feet.
A bed pan in the window of the pharmacy.
After they bandaged his head, they sent him
back to Poland. Radishes in Berlin.
He saves the talles[2] with the silver threads
for the yomim no'roim.[3] When someone enters the
        shop
she straightens her dress. The cat does not
open its eyes at the sound of the bell.
"Before you see me dead," says the mother-
in-law, "I'll see you rot in hell."
The wife of the pharmacist takes a dress
from the cupboard. The widow changed the place
of the chairs in her room. Just the day
for an umbrella not to open. He will see
her legs again in Spring. The bonds were lost

---

1. A passage from the Bible which Jews put on the entrance to their houses.
2. Prayer shawl.
3. The High Holy days.

in the passover cleaning. When he says
"A gitn shabes,"[1] there is a gold tooth
in his mouth. The cat ate a cricket.
In her dead husband's shoe lives a mouse.
After he moves the cupboard he checks to see
if his body passes through the door.
In Alexanderplatz you are allowed to visit neighbors
between two and four. A Purim costume
from last year. On Yom Kippur[2] too
the widow's breasts are large. A blind man's son
leads his father. When he left the synagogue
it was Spring. The stove lights up
the chin of the fishmonger. "Once, almost . . ."
he thinks as she walks by in the street.
The prayer book is made of paper.
"You live," says the butcher, "only once."
When the bank manager is absent, his assistant
sits in his chair. He loves the touch
of the barber's fingers on his hair.
A child wants the stars. The melamed's shadow
ages along with the melamed. He says
"Yes, Yes," but she keeps on giving advice.
The mohel's wife buys cucumbers. The shop clerk
scolds the cabbage on his plate. She fans herself
with a prayer book. Before he became a barber
he was a scribe. The chandelier-seller says "money"
as if it were a holy word. In the bakery shop
a cough is always heard. He remembers carriages.
On Sundays there is a chicken in his stomach.
The dress-seller speaks Jewish also to the
German woman. The butcher yells when they piss

1. "Good Sabbath" (the Sabbath day greeting).
2. The Day of Atonement.

in his yard. One gets up in the morning
and the world exists. One gets up in.
The morning and. The world exists.
The tanner's helper shows the children his tattoo.
When they buried his wife, the beggar
came along too. Before the child was born
her nipples darkened. The gravestone-maker casts
gold dust. The ticket collector acts as if
he were the driver. When one looks at Germans
their facial muscles move. On Yom Kippur
he prays for himself. He explains to her breasts
how to get to the station. A bride no one knows
is in the window of the photography shop.
In the morning the Polish woman's eyes
are red. There will be pushing and shoving
on the day of the resurrection of the dead.

יִג

WHILE EUROPE ROSE UP IN FLAMES, McGREGOR
and Goldstone put together a kind of elegant smoking jacket
made of mohair interwoven with threads of gold, and to the
name of the firm they added the words "Tailors to the
Queen." And for this and other reasons Fred Goldstone was
named president of the English Tailors' Association and became Sir Fred Goldstone. And when McGregor died at a
ripe old age, Sir Goldstone made Gurnisht his partner and
the business changed its name to "Goldstone and Kis, Tailors to the Queen."

And all those years Gurnisht would stare at the backs of men
who walked the streets of London holding a boy by the hand,

and quicken his pace to pass them by, and turn round, and look at their faces, but he never found what he was looking for. Which is why his wife Elizabeth became sad at heart and thought: "Some evil spirit has possessed him. At an age when other men seek a woman to relieve the boredom their wives cause them, he runs about the street looking for a man and a boy."

When they told Gurnisht the war had ended, he bade his father-in-law and his wife goodbye and went to Berlin. And when he arrived there, the odor of smoke filled his nostrils. At first he stayed in a hotel, half of which had been blown up, and at the place where the break had taken place beds and lampshades were exposed to view.

He then went to a Hungarian restaurant where he used to dine to his heart's content in those far-off days. At first he had halaszle, which is a kind of fish soup, in a bowl encircled by purple flowers. He then ate turos teszta, which is a dish of noodles and cheese, in a bowl encircled by purple flowers. Old Kovacs sat at his old table, and by him sat old Balog, and both of them spoke of Franz Josef. And when Gurnisht asked if, by chance, they had run across a tailor from Alexanderplatz named Josef Zilbermann, Kovacs remembered that the Kaiser had sent the Austrians and Hungarians to war in Serbia, and said, "By the time the leaves fall from the trees, the soldiers will be home." And when Gurnisht asked if Alexanderplatz was still standing, Balog said his Imperial Highness the Kaiser was a wise man but this declaration of his contained a touch of rashness. Which is why Gurnisht ordered stewed prunes in a bowl encircled by purple flowers and left.

In the evening Gurnisht went to Alexanderplatz. The old
door was still there, but "Hilde and Sebastian Puckel" was
written on the nameplate. Snow fell. Suddenly it seemed to
Gurnisht that in a world without Joseph and without Yingele
his strength would fail.

In Friedrichstrasse there was one house left standing, and at
the entrance there was a pale light. As Gurnisht entered he
saw that the light was coming from the basement. Gurnisht
went down below ground level and came to a kind of impro-
vised tavern. Next to a counter made of old boards sat a German woman. Cut-Foot and Gouged-Eye sat at a dilapidated
kitchen table and drank spirits. Gurnisht ordered a glass for
himself. The German woman motioned to him with her
hand. Gurnisht sat down next to her. "A visitor to Germany?" the German woman asked. Gurnisht said, "Yes."
Gouged-Eye said to his friend, "The sun and moon are
sealed in large pots." Cut-Foot said, "There is a hole in the
sky." Gouged-Eye said, "Let's invite God to drink." Cut-
Foot said, "He can be talked to only on Thursdays."
Gouged-Eye said, "He comes when you cry." Cut-Foot said,
"He cries himself." Gouged-Eye said, "His head is upside
down. His two bodies are connected." "A visitor who knows
German?" the German woman asked. "Once," Gurnisht
said, "I was in Germany." "America?" the German woman
asked. Gurnisht said, "No." He then drank another glass.
Cut-Foot said, "He is alone in the dark." Gouged-Eye said:
"He is food and drink." Cut-Foot said: "He was hatched
from an egg. He grows out of the ground." Gouged-Eye
said: "He dropped out of his mother's ear." Cut-Foot said:
"When his grandmother saw him she cried." Gouged-Eye
said: "He was born before his time." Cut-Foot said: "He
died of old age." The German woman took another drink.

She had large breasts but her neck was wrinkled. She asked: "What's it like?" and Gurnisht said: "Snow." She corrected herself: "What's it like abroad?" and Gurnisht said "Just like here." The German woman laughed. Gurnisht did not laugh. Cut-Foot said: "He invented wine, got drunk and now he beats his wife." Gouged-Eye said: "He's a card-sharp." Cut-Foot said: "He's a bastard." Gouged-Eye said: "He created the world by spitting." "Do you want to?" said the German woman. Gurnisht said: "Yes." In the bedroom at the end of the tavern the German woman took off her dress, lay down on the floor, spread her legs and said: "Komm." And without knowing what he was doing, Gurnisht came upon her and shouted: "Yisgadal . . . aaah . . . vayiskadash . . . aaah . . . ."[1]

1. Yiddish - "May [His name] be magnified and sanctified," the first two words of the Mourner's Kaddish.

Katschen

KATSCHEN

KATSCHEN[1] DREW A PICTURE OF A WOMAN without any legs. He pulled one of her hairs upwards and curled it around the edge of the page. Then he looked at the woman and thought that her face was a little frightening, but she did not frighten him at all. Still, she might frighten someone who had not drawn her.

Uncle Arthur squeezed the bird's head at the tip of his cane and the skin on his knuckles turned white. "Komm!"[2] he said, and stood up. Once Katschen had seen a cypress swaying in the wind. But that was before his mother had gone up to the sky. He thrust the woman into his trouser pocket and followed Uncle Arthur.

Once they were out of the bank, Uncle Arthur leaned his cane against the window of a bookshop. On the other side of the glass was a stone castle with grey clouds floating about its turrets. Katschen thought the bird could see the tower, and for a moment a sort of happiness for the bird passed through him.

Uncle Arthur placed his hand on Katschen's head and Katschen thought, "Now Uncle Arthur will say 'Verfluchte Welt.'"[3] Uncle Arthur said "Verfluchte Welt," and added, "now Katschen's going to have an ice cream."

Uncle Arthur was normally of the opinion that chocolate or vanilla were the only two colors which might decently be

1. Yiddish - Kitten. (German - Kätzchen.)
2. German - "Come!"
3. German - "Cursed world."

eaten but that day he seemed tired of propriety and bought Katschen a green ice cream studded with different types of nuts.

Katschen first passed his tongue over the ice cream until the twin peaks which rose from the cone had rounded into one. He wore down the mound until the nuts stood out and then he caught them between his teeth. His tongue was cold and his teeth ached with frost. When the mound had been flattened the walls of the cone were exposed and Katschen nibbled around them. All the while, Uncle Arthur's eyes were fixed on the sea. Katschen looked up from the ice cream and asked, "Wohin?"[1] Uncle Arthur withdrew his gaze from the sea and said, "Now we go to another house. Perhaps to Tante[2] Oppenheim."

◈

Aunt Oppenheim was the sister of Katschen's mother and had never married. In Vienna, Aunt Oppenheim had sung in the opera house but in Palestine she sat in the coffeehouse on the seashore and ate cream cakes. Once, she had held Katschen between her legs, pressed his head to her belly and said, "Katschen will not be a swine, nor a schakal[3] like all the others." Since then, a sort of distant memory lingered in Katschen's nostrils and whenever he thought of his life he would see himself walking along a path flanked on either side by swine and jackals. At the end of the path perfume wafted from a silk curtain. Sometimes, when he was unable to sleep, he would place himself on this path and walk along it until he reached the end and was swallowed up in the silk.

1. German - "Where to?"
2. German - Aunt.
3. German - Jackal.

◈

Katschen was about two and a half years old when he first heard that his father was krank.[1] His mother placed a bowl of fruit on the table and walked out of the house. Katschen's father sat silent in the armchair, and when Katschen offered him an apple a tear appeared in the corner of his eye. Katschen opened the doors of the sideboard and arranged the silverware on the carpet. Then he surrounded his father's slippers with the silverware and the feet of the father inside the slippers did not move. After that, Katschen made a habit of asking whether this or that person were krank. By the time he found out other people were nicht krank[2] his father was already in "the institution."

◈

After Katschen's father left there was Herr Druck. He kissed Katschen's mother on both cheeks and asked Katschen, "Vot you learn today?" Katschen's father, who was krank, leaned back against the armchair while Herr Druck leaned forward, with only half his bottom on the armchair. Katschen distinguished between those who were nicht krank and those who were krank. The bodies of the nicht krank were tense while the bodies of the krank were limp. The nicht krank's shoes were black and their socks were pulled up tight, while the krank's feet shone in shades of silver. Herr Druck would come and go and Aunt Oppenheim said to Katschen's mother, "Beware Margarethe. That man is a schakal." Katschen's mother looked at Katschen and said,

---

1. German - sick (here, mentally sick).
2. German - not sick.

"The boy needs somebody." Years later, Katschen read in a book that "There are some animals that resemble dogs, but they are no more than distant relations," and was reminded of Herr Druck.

◈

Aunt Oppenheim opened the door and smiled at Katschen. Katschen wanted to twitch his nostrils and take in the odor of perfume given off by his aunt. Then he decided to wait a little longer until he had walked past her and entered her room.

"Schon wieder hat man uns herausgeschmissen!"[1] said Uncle Arthur, and Aunt Oppenheim said, "Katschen will sleep with me." Then Uncle Arthur and Aunt Oppenheim sipped tea from china cups and Katschen was given raspberry juice in a glass. Katschen compared the color of the raspberry in his glass with the color of the tea in their cups and thought to himself that the color of the tea was only the color of raspberry which had faded. Then he thought that, like their tea, Uncle Arthur and Aunt Oppenheim were children whose color had faded. It had grown dark meanwhile and Aunt Oppenheim lit a yellow lamplight. Shadows danced on the ceiling and Katschen thought up a story at the end of which all the devils died.

When Katschen opened his eyes, he saw a ray of light which stretched from the curtain to the wall opposite. He put his hand into the light and his skin glowed. "Now Katschen will eat porridge," said Aunt Oppenheim, and when she leaned over him her face was white. Katschen considered

---

1. German - "They threw us out again!"

whether he should ask what happened to her face or where Uncle Arthur had gone. "With a lot of sugar," he said.

◇

Suddenly he saw himself in the wardrobe mirror. His body was wrapped in a pink lace nightgown. Katschen brought his face closer to the face in the mirror until his nose touched the nose in the mirror. Then he stuck out his tongue until it touched the tongue in the mirror. "There are two Katschens," he thought. Then he said to himself maybe there were two Aunt Oppenheims as well. In a little while he would sit on the white bench in Aunt Oppenheim's kitchen and eat sweet porridge, and the other Katschen would sit on the other Aunt Oppenheim's kitchen and eat sweet porridge too. When Katschen looked away from the mirror his reflection disappeared. Katschen consoled himself with the thought that the wardrobe mirror was not the real mirror. The mirror in the wardrobe was framed on all sides and images entered it and left it, while the real mirror covered the whole world and there was nothing which it did not double.

"Arthur is already old. Maybe Katschen will live now with Tante Oppenheim. Also Margarethe in the sky wants Katschen to live with Tante Oppenheim," said Aunt Oppenheim. This confused Katschen's thoughts for some time, since he no longer knew where to place the mirror which doubled the world. If he placed it in mid-air it would separate the world below from the world in the sky and hide his mother from him. Katschen decided that the mirror reflected on both its sides and doubled both the worlds—the world below and the world above. But then the fear began to gnaw at him that his double in the mirror would take over his mother in the sky while he himself would only be left with her reflection. Eventually, Katschen decided that the mirror was crystal clear and that even its reflections were real things.

"At night I will sleep here and in the day I will be with Uncle Arthur," said Katschen, and thought to himself that it would be better to eat breakfast with Aunt Oppenheim because her sweet porridge was tastier than Uncle Arthur's bread and margarine. Aunt Oppenheim gave a quiet smile and said, "Uncle Arthur is krank like your father. One day people will find out." Katschen felt a sudden yearning for his uncle and said, "Now I want to go to Uncle Arthur."

Meanwhile, Aunt Oppenheim drew black lines above her eyes and smeared two pink patches on her cheeks. Then she pursed her lips until they formed a ring, and painted them red. Katschen thought to himself that women's faces were white at night and colored in the daytime, while men's faces, which were white during the day, were colored at night. Katschen decided he would look at Uncle Arthur's face at night and see what color it was. "Doesn't Katschen love Tante Oppenheim?" Aunt Oppenheim asked the mirror above her dressing table. Katschen looked at the mirror and waited to see how it would answer. But when he saw that Aunt Oppenheim's eye in the mirror was looking at him, he returned her glance and said, "He does." The eye stared at him and asked, "Katschen loves Uncle Arthur more?" Katschen blushed and did not know what to answer. He suddenly remembered when he had been little and had walked next to Uncle Arthur in the rain, and Uncle Arthur had taken off his coat and wrapped Katschen up in it and carried him close to his chest, and the coat smelled of Uncle Arthur, and Katschen had almost fainted with the pleasure of it.

Katschen looked into the mirror and saw that Aunt Oppenheim's eye was no longer there, and concluded that the time
for an answer had passed.

◈

While Katschen's father was still at home, Uncle Arthur
would come every day when the clock on the wall struck five.
Uncle Arthur sat on the chair next to the table, his face towards Katschen's father. Margarethe touched the shoulder
of Katschen's father in the armchair and said, "Ernst, dein
Bruder ist da."[1] Ernst, who looked at his brother out of the
corner of his eye, shook his head from right to left and said
nothing. A hidden sense told Katschen that the movement of
his father's head was not intended to deny Uncle Arthur but
was a way of saying in krank language: "Ah, my long-limbed
brother, have you come once again to see the face of your
brother whose spirit has been turned inside out?" Uncle
Arthur sipped the chicory which Margarethe placed before
him and spoke to Ernst. He sipped and spoke and Ernst said
nothing. The things Uncle Arthur said to Ernst always began with schon wieder:[2] "Schon wieder autumn has come;"
"Schon wieder I need a walking stick because of the rheuma-
tism;" "Schon wieder the landlord told me to move out of the
room." In the course of time, Katschen understood that the
difference between his father Ernst and his Uncle Arthur lay
in their power to resist this schon wieder. His father had
been beaten by schon wieder, while Uncle Arthur stood up
against it like an old stone wall.

After Ernst was sent to the institution Uncle Arthur

1. German - "Ernst, your brother is here."
2. German - Once again.

would come only once or twice a week. He would suddenly appear at the door, sometimes in the morning and sometimes in the evening, and seat himself in the same chair. Only now the armchair which faced him was empty. Katschen, who knew that Uncle Arthur was staring at the emptiness, would come and stand beside him. Uncle Arthur would sip the chicory Margarethe had put before him and place his hand on Katschen's head. Then he would remove his hand, take another sip, and replace it on Katschen's head. At that moment it seemed to Katschen that Uncle Arthur's resistance to 'schon wieder' had slipped somewhat.

◈

When Aunt Oppenheim had finished painting her face she put on a dress strewn with various flowers and said, "Now Katschen is coming with Tante Oppenheim to the coffeehouse." Katschen inhaled her perfume and Uncle Arthur was forgotten. Outside, the scent of her perfume mingled with the sea salt. Aunt Oppenheim's hand encircled Katschen's like a warm blanket and Katschen was afraid to move it lest Aunt Oppenheim loosen her grip and allow the air to enter between her flesh and his. In her other hand, Aunt Oppenheim held a green handbag. Once she had told Katschen that this bag was made from a crocodile and he was seized with wonder. The crocodile in Katschen's picturebook had a gaping mouth filled with sharp teeth. Katschen often imagined Aunt Oppenheim astride the crocodile, forcing it into submission and turning it into a handbag. When Aunt Oppenheim was in the kitchen, Katschen approached her dressing table and passed his hand over the handbag. "If the crocodile who has turned into a handbag should turn himself back into a crocodile," thought Katschen, "he will devour me in the twinkling of an eye." But the handbag did not turn into a crocodile and Katschen commended himself on his bravery.

On her way to the coffeehouse Aunt Oppenheim nodded to a shopkeeper and to another man. Then a man in a suit placed himself in her path and Aunt Oppenheim let go of Katschen's hand and extended her hand to the man's mouth. The man bowed his head and kissed her hand. Katschen thought to himself that Uncle Arthur greeted people in only one way while Aunt Oppenheim had two ways of greeting them. If they wore faded shirts she nodded to them, but if they wore suits she stretched out her hand to be kissed.

◈

In the coffeehouse red tablecloths fluttered in the wind. Aunt Oppenheim sat herself down by the balcony wall and Katschen sat next to her. Katschen saw black ants going in and out of the wall. A man dressed in white clothes bowed and said, "Guten Morgen, Frau Oppenheim."[1] Katschen thought to himself that the ants in the wall also had a coffeehouse. A white ant was placing two cream cakes on an ant-table and the Aunt-ant was sipping coffee and the Katschen-ant was drinking cocoa from an ant-glass. Aunt Oppenheim wiped the corners of her mouth with a paper serviette and asked, "What is Katschen thinking?" Katschen said, "Ameisen."[2] Aunt Oppenheim stared at Katschen in amazement and said, "Arthur is wrong. Katschen must go to school."

Katschen remembered that Uncle Arthur dressed him in

1. German - "Good morning, Mrs. Oppenheim."
2. German - "Ants."

a white shirt, took his hand and led him to a school with grey
walls and taps in the yard. A woman who smelled of tooth-
paste sat Katschen down at a little wooden table. Katschen
saw that something had been scratched into the table and
read: "SARAH IS MAD." Then the woman put a book in front
of Katschen and told him to copy:

> Higgledy, piggledy, my black hen
> She lays eggs for gentlemen
> Gentlemen come every day

When Katschen came back from school Uncle Arthur
looked at what he had written and said, "Unsinn."[1] During
the break the children would throw a ball to one another and
shout, "Here! Here!" or, "To me! To me!" Katschen stood
under a fig tree and waited for a girl with two black pigtails to
laugh and show her teeth. A few days later, Katschen was ordered to copy something else from the same book:

> To see what my black hen doth lay
> Sometimes nine and sometimes ten
> Higgledy, piggledy, my black hen.

When Uncle Arthur saw what Katschen had written he said
"Unsinn" again and banged the table with his fist. Uncle
Arthur did not send Katschen to school anymore and the
whole affair left Katschen only with a faint feeling of regret
that he had never seen the mad Sarah whose name was on the
table.

Meanwhile, the coffeehouse had filled up with people
and Aunt Oppenheim stretched out her hand to be kissed
three or four times. Katschen saw a big ship sailing in the sea
and looked at it until it disappeared. A boy, a little older than

---

1. German - "Stuff and nonsense."

Katschen, stood below the coffeehouse with a bundle of newspapers under one arm. He waved one newspaper in the air and shouted, "Baat . . . elson . . . Koree . . . Anfront!" Katschen thought to himself that people give names to the days of the year and call each day by a different name, and in order that everyone should know the names of the days, they write them in big black letters on the newspaper and everybody buys them to find out what that day is called. Katschen leaned over the edge of the balcony, looked at the newspaper in the boy's hand and read: BATTLES ON KOREAN FRONT. Katschen asked Aunt Oppenheim, "Was ist 'front'?"[1] Aunt Oppenheim laughed and loosened the top button of her dress. Katschen peeped inside and Aunt Oppenheim said, "But for this Katschen is too little."

Afterwards, a dog ambled up and sat itself down in front of Katschen. Katschen stroked the dog's head and the dog wagged its tail. Katschen gathered the cake crumbs from his plate and offered them to the dog, and the dog stretched out a warm tongue and licked Katschen's palm.

◇

Katschen did not see Uncle Arthur at all that day. In the evening, Aunt Oppenheim undressed him, put him into the bath and washed his whole body. While she was dressing him in the pink nightgown, she told him about a man who used to drive up in a horsedrawn carriage and bring her bouquets of flowers. Katschen asked if they were big horses, and Aunt Oppenheim answered that in this story what was important was not the size of the horse, but the size of the Liebe[2]

1. German - "What does 'front' mean?"
2. German - love.

between herself and that man. Katschen said that when he was big, he too would drive up in a horsedrawn carriage and bring Aunt Oppenheim bouquets of flowers. Aunt Oppenheim kissed Katschen on his forehead and told him that every child has his own special angel which always guards him from harm. Then she taught him a prayer for the angel to come and lead him to the Land of Nod. At night, Katschen dreamed of a big ship sailing across the open sea. Then the ship turned into Aunt Oppenheim, who skimmed across the waves with her dress rolled down to her waist and a garland of flowers around her head.

◇

In the morning, Uncle Arthur arrived with Max the Hungarian. Max's moustache, which was thick underneath his nostrils, grew progressively thinner until it petered out into wispy strands on both sides of his chin. When Katschen saw Uncle Arthur he ran to him and Uncle Arthur lifted him up and pressed him to his chest. Max clicked his heels, took Aunt Oppenheim's hand, bowed his head slightly, and kissed it. From his place against Uncle Arthur's chest, Katschen could see that Aunt Oppenheim's eyes had softened. Max returned Aunt Oppenheim's hand, looked at Katschen and said, "Gozemeber."[1]

Then Uncle Arthur, Aunt Oppenheim and Max sat around the table and drank chicory, and Katschen sat under the table and looked at their shoes. Blue veins extended downwards from Aunt Oppenheim's knees and the flesh of her feet, which were too big for her shoes, bulged out in swollen hillocks. Uncle Arthur's knees were pressed together

---

1. Hungarian - "Rascal."

and his legs were pulled backwards. The tips of his grey
shoes peeped out from under the chair and only his cane was
placed, as a sort of extra limb, under the middle of the table.
One big, black shoe had also situated itself at this point.
Max's other shoe hung in the air between Aunt Oppenheim's legs. Katschen thought to himself that each man puts
on his shoes and is on his way. But then he changed his mind
and decided that each shoe inserts its foot—and the man at
the end of the foot—and is on its way.

Meanwhile the skies outside had darkened and it was
raining. Uncle Arthur said that schon wieder it was winter
and Aunt Oppenheim asked what was going to happen with
the boy. Uncle Arthur said that he, and Max agreed with
him, was of the opinion that schools in Palestine caused
more harm than good and that he and Max would teach him
themselves. Aunt Oppenheim asked Max if he was still with
that schwarze Frau[1] and Max said, "Jawohl."[2] There was silence at tabletop level and Katschen was sorry he couldn't
see Aunt Oppenheim's face from where he was sitting under
the table. Then Aunt Oppenheimn said that the boy thinks
about ants and all he wants to do is look down women's
blouses. Uncle Arthur said the boy was begabt[3] and Max
said that grown-ups don't understand what children are
thinking about at all.

The rain rapped against the windowpanes and Aunt Oppenheim lit the stove. Katschen crawled out from under the
table and sat himself down on Uncle Arthur's knees. He
picked up Uncle Arthur's cane, tapped it on the carpet
around Uncle Arthur's foot, and thought to himself that old

---

1. German - black woman.
2. German - "Yes."
3. German - gifted.

people walk with their legs and support themselves with a stick, while he, Katschen, was not even touching the ground and the stick alone was supporting him. Then Aunt Oppenheim sang what she had once sung in the opera in Vienna and Max sang a song in Hungarian. When he had finished, Max explained to Aunt Oppenheim the meaning of the song: he is sad, and drinks until he can no longer remember his name, but nevertheless women still love him.

◈

Katschen looked at the picture which hung next to Aunt Oppenheim's grandfather clock. In the picture there was a palace and around the palace there were fir trees, and a horse-drawn carriage, and the horse's head was turned towards the palace. The horse's foot hung suspended in mid-air and Katschen waited for the horse to put it down. Then Katschen brought his face up close to the picture and saw that the palace and the trees and the horse had all been embroidered, and remembered that he once saw how Aunt Oppenheim had embroidered a peacock. The peacock was standing on both feet and had already spread its tail, but its face was half in the picture and half in Aunt Oppenheim's spools of cotton. Because of this memory, Katschen thought about Margarethe, his dead mother. She was sitting on the sofa, young and beautiful. In the armchair opposite sat his father, Ernst, while Margarethe embroidered him, Katschen, ever so slowly. At first she embroidered his shoes, then his legs, and his body, and his hands, and his neck. When the thread hung from his neck Margarethe stopped, holding the needle between her thumb and her forefinger, with her three other fingers spread in the air like a bird's wing. "We will make ourselves a beautiful child," she said to Ernst, and

Ernst nodded his head. Then she embroidered Katschen's face and, when she had finished the hair on his head, she cut the thread. "What shall we call the child?" asked Margarethe, and Ernst nodded his head once again. "So be it," said Margarethe, "we shall call him Katschen," and she embroidered the name "Katschen" above the child's head.

Meanwhile, Max the Hungarian had stood up, spread out his arms, and was singing "Meine Liebe ist wie eine Rose."[1] Katschen saw that tears were streaming from Aunt Oppenheim's eyes and remembered the man who drove up in a horse-drawn carriage to bring her bouquets of flowers. That carriage in the picture, thought Katschen, must be this man's, and the palace is Aunt Oppenheim's. She sits in her room in the palace and looks out through the window. Tomorrow, Aunt Oppenheim will take a spool of thread out of her sewing box and embroider the foot of the horse again. And the horse will put its foot down. Then she will embroider the feet of the horse as they rise and fall until the horse reaches the gates of the palace. And when the horse reaches the gates of the palace she will embroider the man descending from the carriage and offering her flowers.

◈

As they walked away from Aunt Oppenheim's house Uncle Arthur held one of Katschen's hands and Max the Hungarian held the other. The rain had stopped and grey clouds sailed towards Katschen, Uncle Arthur and Max the Hungarian and passed over their heads. "If Uncle Arthur and Max the Hungarian had chosen to lead me to where the clouds are sailing," thought Katschen, "the wind would

1. German - "My Love Is Like a Rose."

carry them up and they would float in the sky." As they walked down the steps to the sea, Max said, "Eins, zwei, drei—hops!" and Uncle Arthur and Max lifted Katschen up, carried him through the air for a distance, and put him back down on his feet. When Katschen was in the air he saw the sea, and when Uncle Arthur and Max put him down, the sea disappeared. It seemed to Katschen that it was the sea, and not him, which rose and appeared, sank and disappeared.

When they arrived at the bottom of the steps, the sea stood still and spread out before them. Uncle Arthur dropped Katschen's hand, placed both his hands on the bird's head, and leaned his body against the cane. Katschen saw that the tip of Uncle Arthur's cane was sinking into the sand and the fear stole up on him that the sand would suck Uncle Arthur under, into the earth, and he, Katschen would be left alone on its surface. But Uncle Arthur pulled his cane out of the sand, and held Katschen's hand again.

Katschen lifted his eyes and noticed that they were standing near a hut smeared with tar paper. Out of the window of the hut peered a head with gold-rimmed spectacles on its nose and a white beard hanging from its chin. The head moved from one shoulder to the other, and said, "Oy vey! Oy vey!" Max the Hungarian looked at the head and said, "Guten Tag, Herr Schneider."[1] The head moved once more from one shoulder to the other and said, "Oy vey, oy vey, and vot is so good about such a day?" Max the Hungarian laughed and said, "Herr Lumpenschneider,[2] this is Katschen. Now Katschen is also Lumpenprolet."[3] Then he grabbed Katschen and lifted him onto his head. From his seat on Max's head Katschen saw that the head in the win-

1. German - "Good day, Mr. Tailor."
2. German - "Mister Tattered-Tailor."
3. German - lumpen proletariat.

dow was attached to a body—and that the body was sitting in front of a sewing machine. "A good boy, a good boy," said the tailor. Max said, "not just a boy. This is a prinz.[1] And now Prinz Katschen is coming to the palace of King Max." Katschen remembered that Max's eyes were blue-green and thought that Max was King of the Sea, who sits on the beach and looks at the sea all day long. When his eyes are blue—the sea is blue, and when his eyes are green—the sea is green.

Max turned away from the tailor and entered an alleyway which ran between the huts. Now the wind blew against their backs and the clouds came up behind them and drifted into the distance. Katschen turned round and saw that Uncle Arthur was leaning forwards, as though the bird on his cane had spread its wings and was pulling his long body upwards.

◆

Max lifted Katschen down from his head. Then he brought his two fists in front of his mouth like a bugle and called out, "Avigail, Avigail, open up the palace. Emperor Franz-Joseph, the King of Hungary and the Little Prince are here!"

At the door of the hut appeared a woman with dark skin and black hair. She stared at Katschen, pointed a brown finger in his direction and said, "Ooooo aa! Ooooo aa! This must be Arthur's nephew. Welcome to my humble abode. Avigail will call you Pussycat!" Katschen looked into Avigail's black eyes and thought to himself that she was a sort of hexe[2] who used spells and turned children into animals.

Avigail sat Katschen down at a table and placed a bowl before him which gave off white steam. Katschen thought to

1. German - prince.
2. German - witch.

himself that there was magic potion in the bowl and when he drank it, he would turn into a cat. But the bowl also smelled of meat and pepper and Katschen swallowed the potion down to the last drop.

The sun stood in the window of the hut like a red wheel. "When the wheel of the sun sinks down into the sea," thought Katschen to himself, "I will be no more." His eyelids were heavy and through his eyelashes he could make out Avigail's figure, close by and far away, far away and close by. When she picked him up in her arms he closed his eyes and remembered the angel Aunt Oppenheim had told him about. "This angel," thought Katschen, "is smooth skinned, and smells of wild grass, and will always guard me from harm."

At night, Katschen heard voices and opened his eyes. Rain beat down on the roof of the hut. Uncle Arthur stood at the window, looking out to sea. From the bed at the other end of the hut rose Max's voice, "Jesus Christus! Jesus Christus! Jesus Cristus!" he cried. And Avigail's voice answered him, "Ooooo aa! Ooooo aa! Ooooo aa!" Katschen strained his eyes and saw that the bodies of Max the Hungarian and Avigail were going up and down, up and down. Uncle Arthur walked over to Katschen, covered him with a blanket up to his chin and said, "Schlaff meine kind, schlaff!"[1] Water streamed down the windowpanes. Then Max and Avigail fell silent and Katschen lay for a long time listening to the voice of the rain and imagining that he was turning into a cat.

◇

In the morning Uncle Arthur was standing by the window facing the sea. Katschen remembered what he had seen in

---

1. German - "Sleep my child, sleep."

the night and looked at the bed at the other end of the hut. In the bed lay only Max, his mouth gaping wide. At that moment, Avigail appeared in the doorway with some herbs in her hand. "Does Pussycat like na'ana?"[1] she asked. Katschen, who did not know what na'ana was, nodded his head and said, "Ja." Avigail placed some earth-colored tea before him, suspended her fingers in the steam which rose from it, and let the herbs drop. The herbs sunk down to the bottom of the cup like a sort of forest on the sea bed. "Drink, Pussycat, drink," said Avigail, and watched Katschen with black eyes. As he sipped at the drink, Katschen lowered his eyes to see whether cat's fur had already begun to grow on his hands. Then Avigail placed before him a sort of round bread sprinkled with small seeds. As the bread was hard, Katschen dipped it into the cup and saw that the end of the bread was peeking through the herbage like a fish head. Katschen chewed the bread and thought to himself, "Pussycat eats fish." But when he looked at Avigail again, she was plaiting her hair and her lips were smiling. "Arrturr," said Avigail. The sound of Uncle Arthur's name rolled around her mouth like a train on iron tracks. "I'm going out with the boy to the beach." Uncle Arthur did not turn away from the window.

Black crows jumped on the sand. The sea was green but the sky was cloudless and the light blue. Avigail slipped off her shoes, held them in one hand and held out her other hand to Katschen. Katschen saw that Avigail's feet were brown, and remembered Aunt Oppenheim's foot which was white with the little toe bent inwards and covered by a sort of thick crust. Avigail's toes were all straight, and along the sole of her foot ran a kind of line which divided the brown skin above from the white skin below. Katschen felt the urge to

1. Arabic - mint.

touch Avigail's feet, and without wanting to, and without knowing why, suddenly said, "Jesus Christus."

◈

Max said, "Now I tell from the beginning. Mah ze chaim?[1] What is life?" Katschen was reminded of Chaim Heiventreiger who used to throw four stones up in the air. As the stones were on their way up, Chaim Heiventreiger would pick up another stone which he had placed on the ground, turn his hand palm up, and catch the stones he had thrown up as they came down. Once Chaim Heiventreiger's parents moved to Jaffa, Katschen never saw him again.

"You think," continued Max, "that life is gas, and then amoeba, and then fish, and then fish which come out of the water with legs, and then monkey and then man. Life is not gas, not amoeba, not fish, not fish with legs, not monkey. Katschen hear the music of Liszt[2] and understand life. Max with woman—Max understand. Life is secret, life is secret," said Max twice, and fell silent. Katschen remembered what he had seen the night before and thought to himself that the stones which Chaim Heiventreiger throws go up only once, while Max and Avigail go up because they come down and come down because they go up. The same thought persisted in his mind until it took on the form of a picture. Black crows jump on the beach. Avigail, swathed in a white robe, floats barefoot across the sand. And out of the water walks a fish with four legs and the face of Chaim Heiventreiger. He throws four stones into the air, catches them in his hand and calls after Avigail, "Wanna try? Wanna try?"

1. Hebrew - What is life?
2. Franz Liszt - Hungarian composer (1811–1886) who included gypsy melodies in his compositions.

◇

Then Max walked over to a box in the corner of the hut, placed a sort of handle inside it, turned it seven times and said, "Arthur soldat[1] of Franz-Joseph. Max soldat of Franz Liszt. Katschen know what is Zigeuner?[2] Zigeuner steal chickens and make beautifullest music. This, teacher in school not know. He know only liberation of Jews. Music is liberation of man."

From the box came the sounds of a melody which rose higher and higher. Then it fell down, down, and then up and down, up and down. The sounds sent Katschen spinning round and round. They entered his ears, his mouth, his nostrils, and sent a shudder through his chest and stomach. At first, Katschen saw a man with a drooping moustache drawing a violin bow across the back of a large rooster. Then the man disappeared and the rooster flew slowly up into the darkness. Thousands of birds circled the sky. The birds' wings were on fire and the sound of their voices reached from one end of the world to the other.

Then the music came to an end and Katschen saw tears running down the cheeks of Max the Hungarian. Katschen thought to himself that Max was crying over the birds that burned. He looked at Uncle Arthur and saw that his eyes were clear. Katschen climbed onto Uncle Arthur's lap and clung to his chest. Uncle Arthur stroked Katschen's head and said, "Genug,[3] Max."

In the afternoon, the tailor with gold-rimmed spectacles on his nose came and sat at the table. Avigail placed a bowl of soup in front of him and the tailor bent forward and put his

1. German - soldier.
2. German - gypsy.
3. German - enough.

beard in the steam. Then he raised the bowl to his lips, took a sip of soup and said, "Nu nu!"[1] Max looked at him, his eyes aflame, and said, "Nu nu ist gar nichts."[2] The tailor looked at Max and said, "Gurnisht is gurnisht."[3] Max said, "Nu nu is gurnisht." The tailor said, "What have you got against me today?" Max made no reply. The tailor turned to Uncle Arthur and said, "Nu?"[4] Uncle Arthur rested his chin on his hand and said, "Nu nu ist etwas."[5] The tailor smiled with satisfaction. Max fixed his eyes on Uncle Arthur and said, "Was ist nu nu?"[6] Uncle Arthur tugged at the end of his chin and said, "Nu nu ist alles."[7] Max said, "Alles ist gar nichts."[8] The tailor said, "Gurnisht is gurnisht."[9] Max said, "Nu nu is gurnisht." The tailor said, "Nu nu." Katschen remembered that his mother, Margarethe, used to look at his father and say, "Ja ja," and was filled with affection for the tailor.

◇

At night Katschen had a dream. A wild-haired woman set the forest on fire and Max ran after her shouting, "I am King of the World! I am King of the World!" High above floated a large grandfather clock whose face was the face of the tailor. The hands of the clock were gold-rimmed spectacles and the pendulum beneath it was a white beard. And at the edge of

---

1. Yiddish - "Well well": a world-weary sigh common among Eastern European Jews.
2. German - "Nu nu is nothing."
3. Yiddish - "No thing is nothing."
4. Yiddish - "Well?" (meaning, "What do you think?")
5. German - "Nu nu is something."
6. German - "What is nu nu?"
7. German - "Nu nu is everything."
8. German - "Everything is no thing."
9. Yiddish - "No thing is nothing."

the picture was Uncle Arthur leaning on his cane and saying, "This is mad Sarah."

When Katschen woke the next morning the sky was grey and the sea was stormy. Max sat at the table, his face somber, and Avigail stood in the corner of the hut with her face to the paraffin stove and her back to Katschen. Uncle Arthur saw that Katschen's eyes were open and sat down next to him on the edge of the bed. Katschen asked Uncle Arthur, "Sind alle Frauen verrückt?"[1] Uncle Arthur smiled and said, "Nein." Then he told Katschen in German that Margarethe, his mother, had been a beautiful woman in her youth. "Margarethe chose Ernst," he said, "because he was the more stubborn. But Ernst was afraid to lose her and went out of his mind. Women are not mad, but neither are they sane. Only men go in and out of their minds because of the women."

Katschen remembered that he had once heard his father speak. Suddenly, Ernst had lifted up his head and said, "Warum?"[2] in a deep voice. Margarethe rested her hands on Ernst's shoulders and said, "Alles ist in Ordnung Ernst, alles ist in Ordnung."[3]

Then Uncle Arthur told Katschen that if it hadn't been for Zionism he would have married Gertrud, who was not as beautiful as Margarethe, but always knew the right thing to do. But because of Zionism he traveled to Palestine and Gertrud remained in Vienna. But even if he had stayed in Vienna, Gertrud might not have married him since Gertrud believed in three Gods while he (like all the Jews) believed only in one.

1. German - "Are all women mad?"
2. German - "Why?"
3. German - "Everything is in order, Ernst, everything is in order."

All the while, Avigail had been quietly humming to her-self by the paraffin stove. When Uncle Arthur fell silent Katschen could hear Avigail's song curl like cotton wool clouds and spin itself out in a wail, "Ya howwa ya howwa." Avigail suddenly looked at Katschen and said, "Howwa is the wind." Katschen saw that Avigail's cheeks had reddened as though on fire. "Ana wa'inta fi ilhowwa min zar'ina sowwa ya howwa, ya howwa, ya howwa, ya howwa,"[1] sang Avigail. "This is a song of two children in the desert," she said to Katschen, and then she looked at Max, and Katschen under-stood from her eyes that the child Avigail had loved in the desert was not Max.

◈

Katschen looked at Max's face and saw that he had no eye in his forehead. Once Margarethe had told Katschen about Cyclopes.[2] "He who sees with two eyes," she said, "closes one eye when the sights he sees are painful. If he is also pained by the sights he sees with the eye that remains open—he closes both eyes. But the Cyclops never closes his one and only eye." On hearing this, Katschen closed one eye and saw that there was not a great deal of difference be-tween the sights he saw with one eye and the sights he saw with two. Then he closed the eye that remained open and thought to himself, "Now I will never see anything ever again." But then, when his eyes were closed, an eye in his forehead opened. The sight he saw with this eye was not clear, but it held a kind of transparency missing from the

1. Arabic - "I and thee in the wind from our childhood together."
2. In Greek mythology the Cyclopes were a race of giants who had only one eye in the center of their foreheads.

sights he saw with his other two eyes. When Katschen looked in the mirror he could not find the eye in his forehead, but when he closed his eyes again he knew for sure that the eye was there. Since that day, Katschen knew that he was a Cyclops and would look at people to see if they had an eye in their foreheads.

Once Herr Druck, who used to come to Margarethe, said, "Call me Zelig. All right?" Katschen felt the eye in his forehead opening. He closed his eyes and saw that Herr Druck did not see him, Katschen, at all, and was speaking to Margarethe alone. But the Margarethe Herr Druck was speaking to was not Margarethe his mother, who was thin and chewed her fingernails, but a full-bodied Margarethe whose fingers were painted red. Katschen opened his eyes and said, "Zelig." Herr Druck said, "That's good. That's good." Katschen looked at Margarethe, his mother, and saw that she too was a Cyclops but what the eye in her forehead saw pained her and she closed this eye and opened her other two eyes.

Katschen understood that Ernst, his father, was also a Cyclops. But Ernst was no more than a Cyclops and could only see through the eye in his forehead. If Herr Druck had been swallowed up inside my father, thought Katschen to himself, Ernst too would have been able to see like other people, and they would not have sent him to the institution. Katschen felt pity for Herr Druck who ran to and fro between Margarethe and himself and did not know that they were Cyclopes. Later, when Herr Druck had dwindled and faded away, Katschen was sorry. He was not sorry because of Herr Druck, but because of the eyes which Herr Druck had and his father did not have. Once Katschen said "Zelig" a hundred times and hoped in his heart that the word had the power to reach the institution.

◇

Meanwhile, Avigail had placed herb tea on the table and bread sprinkled with seeds. Max sipped the tea but did not reach for the bread and his face was as somber as before. Outside the sea raged. Suddenly, Uncle Arthur said, "Kant."[1] Max raised his head and said, "Keren Kayemet."[2] Uncle Arthur looked at Max and said, "Heine."[3] Max looked at Uncle Arthur and said "Kofer ha-Yishuv."[4] Uncle Arthur said, "Franz-Joseph." Max said, "Franz Liszt." Uncle Arthur said, "Arlozorov."[5] Max said, "Shenkin."[6] Uncle Arthur said, "Schinken,"[7] and they both laughed. Avigail laughed too. Katschen saw that everyone was laughing, and laughed as well.

"Wo ist Katschen?"[8] Aunt Oppenheim's silhouette stood in the doorway of the hut like two umbrellas joined together. "Two days," said Aunt Oppenheim, "I am worrying about Katschen." "Komm herein,"[9] Uncle Arthur said, but Aunt Oppenheim stared at Max and Avigail and did not budge. Sun entered the cabin round Aunt Oppenheim's head and between her legs. Katschen went up to her and pressed his head against her stomach. Aunt Oppenheim's stomach was soft and her dress smelled of perfume. Uncle Arthur got up from his chair, took his cane and went outside. Aunt Oppenheim took hold of Katschen's hand and followed

---

1. German philosopher.
2. Hebrew - Jewish National Fund.
3. German-Jewish poet.
4. Hebrew - Tax paid by Jewish residents of Palestine.
5. Chaim Arlozorov - Jewish Palestinian Labor leader.
6. Menachem Shenkin - Zionist leader and one of the founders of Tel Aviv.
7. German - Ham.
8. German - "Where is Katschen?"
9. German - "Come in."

Uncle Arthur. Katschen saw that for every step which Uncle Arthur took, Aunt Oppenheim took two, and thought to himself that people walk the way their hearts beat. Uncle Arthur, whose heart beat slowly, walked slowly and took long steps, while Aunt Oppenheim, whose heart beat quickly, took short steps.

At the end of the alleyway the head of the tailor peered out of the window. "A giten tug,"[1] said the tailor's head and added, "Ist die gnädige Frau ihre Schwester?"[2] Uncle Arthur heard the tailor speak German and looked at him in amazement. The tailor removed his head from the window, appeared at the doorway of the hut and presented his entire body to Aunt Oppenheim. "Ich war in Wien,"[3] said the tailor. Aunt Oppenheim's eyes softened and she nodded her head. The tailor said, "Meine Frau ist gestorben."[4] Aunt Oppenheim looked into the tailor's face and smiled. The tailor extended both hands towards the interior of the hut and said, "Kommen sie herein af a gleisl tee."[5] Aunt Oppenheim's eyes which had softened now hardened again. She looked away from the tailor and said, "Es tut mir leid."[6]

Katschen pondered what Aunt Oppenheim had said. At first he thought Aunt Oppenheim's sorrow came about because the tailor's wife had died. Then he thought Aunt Oppenheim's sorrow was not because of the tailor's dead wife but because she didn't want his cup of tea. As he was thinking these thoughts a picture emerged in his mind. The tailor

1. Yiddish - "Good day."
2. German - "Is the good lady your sister?"
3. German - "I was in Vienna."
4. German - "My wife passed away."
5. "Please come in for a cup of tea." The beginning of this sentence is in German and the end is in Yiddish.
6. German - "I am sorry." (literally—It causes me sorrow.)

sits next to a sewing machine in front of the window. His wife who died approaches him with a cup of tea in her hand. The tailor sips the tea which his dead wife puts in front of him and the lenses of his spectacles steam over. His fingers extricate a slice of lemon from the tea. He sucks the lemon between his lips and says, "Nu nu." This picture made Katschen feel a sorrow of his own for the tailor and Aunt Oppenheim's sorrow was forgotten.

◈

Uncle Arthur and Aunt Oppenheim held Katschen's hands and walked down the steps to the sea. Katschen remembered how Uncle Arthur and Max the Hungarian had led him down the same steps and lifted him up in the air and how it seemed that the sea, and not he, rose and fell. "Now," thought Katschen, "the sea doesn't rise and doesn't fall, it stands still." As soon as Uncle Arthur and Aunt Oppenheim came to the beach they let go of Katschen's hands and turned to each other. Uncle Arthur said that Katschen should be bei mir[1] while Aunt Oppenheim disagreed and said that Katschen should be bei mir.

Katschen saw a shell. Once his mother Margarethe told him that shells contained the sound of the sea, and even if the shell was far away from the sea, in the mountains, or the desert, the sound of the waves is always in it. Katschen lifted the shell to his ear. The sound of the sea came out of the shell and seemed to Katschen to be saying "bei mir, bei mir." Katschen looked at the sea and saw a ray of light descending from the sky and painting a slice of the sea gold. Once Uncle Arthur had pointed far out to sea and said, "Dort ist

1. German - with me.

Zypern."[1] Katschen thought to himself that Zypern was a land of gold and that the people who lived in the sky went down that ray of light and came to Zypern.

"Onkel Arthur and Tante Oppenheim want Katschen to go to a good place," said Aunt Oppenheim. "Now," thought Katschen, "I'll sail in a ship to Zypern and there I'll meet Margarethe." A wave of joy rose from his stomach and spread through his chest. "To Zypern? To Zypern?" asked Katschen, and Aunt Oppenheim said, "To kibbutz."[2]

◇

When Katschen and Uncle Arthur came back from the sea, the tailor's head was back in the window. "Women," said the head, "are the work of the devil." But Uncle Arthur held tight to Katschen's hand and said nothing.

That evening, Uncle Arthur packed Katschen's clothes into a suitcase. Avigail placed Katschen's socks on her knees, threaded a darning needle and quietly hummed, "Ya howwa, ya howwa." Max sat at the table with an angry face. "Arthur," said Max. Uncle Arthur raised his head from the suitcase and looked at Max. "Warum kibbutz?"[3] asked Max. Uncle Arthur returned his gaze to the suitcase and was silent. Then Uncle Arthur took Katschen's shoes and polished them with brown polish. "Arthur," said Max, "you cannot repair a big evil with a little good." But Uncle Arthur did not raise his head. Katschen was suddenly filled with longing. He looked at Uncle Arthur, who was stooped over

1. German - "There is Cyprus."
2. Hebrew - A collective farm run on socialist principles. Kibbutzim sometimes absorb homeless children.
3. German - "Why kibbutz?"

his shoes, and understood that this longing was for Uncle Arthur, and was filled with amazement that he could long for Uncle Arthur even though he was right next to him.

◈

That night Katschen had a dream. But by the morning, when Uncle Arthur woke him up, he had forgotten it. Avigail smiled at Katschen, placed an apple in his hand and said, "Goodbye, pussycat." Uncle Arthur picked up the suitcase and said, "Komm, mein Kind."[1]

The moon still lit the sky. The tailor's window was shut but Katschen could see light through the blinds, and the tailor's shadow moved along the opposite wall. "A man's shadow," thought Katschen, "lives inside his body at night, and in the daytime the shadow comes out of the body and walks behind him. A shadow is also a kind of man, and a man's name is also his shadow's name. The tailor has a shadow and its name is 'Schneider,' Uncle Arthur has a shadow and its name is 'Uncle Arthur,' and Katschen also has a shadow and its name is 'Katschen.' "

By the time they reached the bus stop the moon had gone away and it was daylight. A woman was sitting at one end of the bus, and a man at the other with a swollen neck. Katschen looked at the man's neck and thought to himself that the man's shadow also had a swollen neck.

After the bus had left the city streets Katschen looked at Uncle Arthur and saw that his head was bent forward but his eyes saw nothing. Uncle Arthur's cane leaned against the window and the bird's head faced the fields.

1. German - "Come, my child."

◈

As Uncle Arthur and Katschen entered the gate of the kibbutz Uncle Arthur turned to a man dressed in blue clothes
and asked where he could find Herr Grossman. The man
pointed to a house and said, "In the office." Uncle Arthur
held Katschen's hand and set off towards the house the man
had pointed to.

Suddenly, Katschen saw a cow. Katschen looked into the
cow's eyes and the cow looked into Katschen's eyes. Since
Katschen had come to a halt, Uncle Arthur rested his cane
against the fence of the cattle pen, and stood still. Then
Uncle Arthur picked up his cane again, took Katschen's
hand and said, "Komm, mein Kind." As they were leaving
Katschen looked back and saw that the cow had also turned
its head and was looking at him.

Herr Grossman was not in the house but a woman there
told Uncle Arthur Herr Grossman was not a Herr[1] at all, and
there wasn't a single Herr on the kibbutz, since everyone
who came to the kibbutz left the Herr outside. Katschen
wondered where the Herr was stuck to this Grossman and
how he removed it when he arrived at the kibbutz. Then
the woman looked at Katschen and asked, "And what's
your name?" Katschen said, "Katschen." The woman said,
"That's a suitable name for Germany. Here we'll have to call
you by a name that's suitable for a kibbutz." Katschen remembered Avigail and wanted to tell the woman his name
was "Pussycat" but from her face he undertstood that
"Pussycat" was not a suitable name for a kibbutz either.

---

1. Kibbutz members have adopted the practice of addressing each other as
"chaver" (comrade) instead of "Mr."

Meanwhile, Herr Grossman had arrived and said, "This is the boy?" Then he looked at Katschen and said, "And what's your name?" Katschen was silent. Herr Grossman asked Uncle Arthur, "Doesn't he speak Hebrew?" "He does," said Uncle Arthur, "but his name is not right for a kibbutz." Herr Grossman asked, "And what is his name?" Uncle Arthur said, "Katschen." Herr Grossman said, "You're right, that's not a proper name for a kibbutz. Let's go to the school."

Herr Grossman walked out of the house and Uncle Arthur and Katschen followed him. Outside, a man in blue rode past Katschen on a bike. The wind blew. When they passed the cattle pen the cow was standing there looking at Katschen. Katschen looked into the cow's eyes and said, "Ich bin Katschen!"[1]

◈

At the door of the school Uncle Arthur patted Katschen's head and said, "Mein kind." Then he turned his back and walked towards the gate of the kibbutz, and it seemed to Katschen as though Uncle Arthur's cane was groping its way along the path like a blind man's stick.

Herr Grossman placed his hand on Katschen's back and led him into a room. "The new boy," said Herr Grossman. Children with untidy hair and a man holding a sort of carving knife immediately stared at Katschen. The man put down the carving knife and said, "Good. And what's your name?" Herr Grossman said, "I'll talk to you about that later." The man looked curiously at Katschen and said, "Sit down." Katschen sat down. The man picked up the carving

1. German - "I'm Katschen!"

knife again and, with his other hand, took a green leaf from the table. Then he looked Katschen in the face and said, "Since city dwellers have distanced themselves from nature, nature has distanced herself from them. Have you ever heard of photosynthesis?" Katschen thought the man was talking to him in German and said, "Nein." The children laughed. The man said, "Don't you speak Hebrew?" "No. Yes," said Katschen. The children laughed again. The man looked angrily at Katschen and said, "The leaf absorbs sunlight and turns it into chlorophyll." Then he cut the leaf with his carving knife, turned back to Katschen and said, "Have you ever seen a leaf through a magnifying glass?" Behind Katschen's back one of the children called out, "Nein," and they all laughed for the third time. The man smiled and said, "Children, we must give the new member a warm welcome." Then all the children looked at the leaf through a magnifying glass, but Katschen, whose eyes were filled with tears, saw nothing.

When the children went out into the yard they clustered around Katschen. One pointed at Katschen's shirt, which was buttoned up to his collar, and asked why he wasn't wearing a tie. Another said that Katschen's coat was funny. Katschen turned his head and walked away. By the side of a road, near a tree, he saw a ladder. He lifted his eyes to see what was at the top, and saw a woman in blue. The woman had a saw in her hand and was cutting down branches. "The work of the people in this place," thought Katschen, "is cutting. Some of them carry carving knives and cut leaves, and some of them carry saws and cut branches." Katschen remembered that when Herr Grossman came to the kibbutz they cut off his Herr. "Soon, when the people here turn to me," thought Katschen to himself, "they will cut my name off." And as Katschen thought of his name, he remembered the cow. He walked along the paths of the kibbutz to the cattle pen to see the cow, but the cow was not there. Katschen raised his eyes and saw green fields lying beyond the kibbutz. He left the kibbutz and walked into the fields to look for the cow.

◈

When his mother died, Aunt Oppenheim told Katschen that Margarethe had gone up to the sky and this statement seemed right to him. Once Katschen saw Uncle Arthur reading a book. Katschen stood behind him and looked at the picture in the book. In a field, inside a pit, stood a man with an ugly face holding a skull in his hand. Katschen asked Uncle Arthur, "Was ist das?"[1] and Uncle Arthur said, "Der Tote von gestern und der Tote von morgen,"[2] and this statement of Uncle Arthur's seemed right as well. "The dead," thought Katschen, "go out into the fields, fall slowly on their faces and the earth covers them. Then slowly they break through the earth and go up to the sky."

Now grass soaked Katschen's trousers and mud covered the shoes which Uncle Arthur had polished. Clouds covered the sky. In the middle of the field stood a man surrounded by sheep. The man looked at Katschen, but Katschen, who was looking for the cow, continued on his way.

At the edge of the field Katschen saw a ditch with a stream running along the bottom. When Katschen climbed down into the ditch a big crab was startled and ran into the water. Before the crab disappeared Katschen saw on its back two eyes looking at him. Then Katschen wandered along the

---

1. German - "What is that?"
2. German - "The dead of yesterday and the dead of tomorrow."

side of the stream until he saw a tree trunk half in and half out of the water. Katschen climbed onto the tree trunk and walked, step by step, across the stream. When he was half-way across, the tree trembled and Katschen's body trembled with it. But then Katschen heard the lowing of a cow. His body straightened and he crossed over to the other side of the stream. As Katschen climbed up out of the ditch the shadow of a mountain was spread across the fields. "In a little while," thought Katschen, "I'll find the cow. Then I'll fall on my face and the earth of the field will cover me."

◈

"Mutti,"[1] said Katschen. But when the sound of his voice reached his ears, it seemed as though the word had not come out of his mouth. "Mutti," said Katschen again, but it was as though his lips were not his own. "Howw . . . ," blew the wind, "waa . . . ," blew the wind. Katschen listened to the sound of the wind and remembered Avigail's song. "Howwa" is the sound of the wind and "howwa" is the name of the wind, thought Katschen. When the wind blows you hear its name and when you hear its name it blows. "Wi—ind," said Katschen. "Wi—ind," and this word too sounded to Katschen like the sound of the wind.

And as things and the names of things became one, the fear in Katschen's heart disappeared. "Mutti," he said for the third time, and this time the voice was his own and the lips were his own. "Have you lost your way, my son?" Katschen heard Margarethe say. "Ja," answered Katschen, "I have lost my way." But there was no doubt in Katschen's mind that he would soon find his way, and follow it until he reached the

---

1. German - "Mama."

cow. And the cow would look into Katschen's eyes and say, "There, you have found your way, mein kind, and you need never stray so far again."

"Min hadda?"[1] said a voice from out of the darkness, and metal clicked against metal. A black shadow approached Katschen. "Min inti?"[2] said the shadow. Katschen saw that the shadow had the face of an old man with a large moustache on both sides of his nose and white hair covering his chin. When the old man saw Katschen's face he hung the rifle over his shoulder and said, "Min neyn jit?"[3] But Katschen looked at the old man's face and said nothing. The old man also looked at Katschen's face and remained silent. The old man and Katschen looked at each other for a long time.

Then the old man turned his back on Katschen and walked away. His figure was swallowed up in the field but the barrel of his gun stuck up and moved across the clouds. "That gun," thought Katschen to himself, "is Uncle Arthur's cane with the bird at the top, and the bird is turning its head and looking at me."

Katschen picked up his feet and ran after the bird. "Onkel Arthur," cried Katschen, "Onkel Arthur?" The bird appeared and disappeared between the clouds. Katschen's shoes tangled in the weeds and his legs hurt. "To the sky," thought Katschen, "to the sky. Birds fly to the sky. Margarethe is in the sky. Uncle Arthur is in the sky." Suddenly Katschen's body seemed as light as a bird and he was floating above the earth. "At last," thought Katschen, and closed his eyes.

1. Arabic - "Who's that?"
2. Arabic - "Who are you?"
3. Arabic - "Where are you from?"

◇

When Katschen opened his eyes, he saw the old man standing over him. A black robe covered his body and on his head he wore a cloth kerchief tied with black rope. Katschen looked around and saw a tent made out of black sheets. In the corner of the tent embers were glowing and on the embers stood a kettle. When the old man saw Katschen looking at him, he offered him some thin round bread and said, "Kol."[1] Katschen took the bread from the old man's hand and chewed at it. Then he raised his head and saw that he was lying on a mattress scattered with cushions. The old man hunched down with his legs tucked under him and his haunches brushing the floor. He laid his hands on his knees and looked at Katschen.

Katschen ate. From time to time the twigs on the fire crackled, and black shadows leaped across the flaps of the tent. The old man rose from his place and handed Katschen tea that smelled of flowers.

Suddenly, it seemed to Katschen that he had once been in this place, and had once eaten what he was eating, and the old man had once sat like that and looked at him. "Never," thought Katschen, "will I have to leave this place again." His eyes felt heavy and through half-shut lids he saw the old man standing over him with a woolen blanket in his hands. "Nam,"[2] said the old man and pressed lightly on Katschen's shoulder. Katschen lay back on the mattress and folded his legs into his stomach. The old man spread the blanket over Katschen's body and tucked the sides into the mattress. Before Katschen closed his eyes he saw the old man take the

1. Arabic - "Eat."
2. Arabic - "Sleep."

kettle and pour himself some bitter-smelling coffee into a tiny china cup.

◇

"Komm,"[1] said Uncle Arthur and shook Katschen's shoulder. Katschen opened his eyes and saw the face of the old man. "The old man," thought Katschen, "is a kind of Uncle Arthur. Sometimes he talks in Uncle Arthur's language and sometimes in another language."

The old man placed a glass of milk in front of Katschen. Katschen drank the milk and it was very sweet. The tent smelled of morning dew and other, more pungent smells which Katschen had never smelled before. "Nimshi,"[2] said the old man. "Nimshi," thought Katschen, "is a word with a beautiful sound. When I meet Uncle Arthur again I'll teach him this word."

The old man walked out of the tent and Katschen followed. Outside Katschen saw a donkey. Katschen looked the donkey in the face, and the donkey looked like the eyes of the cow that Katschen went to look for in the fields. Black goats stood in a stockade made of dry branches and looked at Katschen. "Ziegen,"[3] said Katschen to the old man. The old man gripped Katschen's waist and sat him on the back of the donkey. Then he took up the rope tied around the donkey's neck and led the donkey into the fields. Katschen turned round and saw that the goats were still looking at him. When the old man reached the edge of the field he led the donkey for some while along a path which ran between two fields. The old man climbed up a hill and the donkey climbed after

1. German - "Come"; Arabic - "Arise."
2. Arabic - "Let us go."
3. German - "Goats."

him. When the donkey reached the top of the hill the old man gripped Katschen's waist and lifted him down to the ground. At the foot of the hill Katschen saw little red-roofed houses. The old man pointed to the houses and said, "Yahud."[1] Then, he removed from his neck a little horn which hung from a thread, and placed it around Katschen's neck. "Ma ee-saleme,"[2] said the old man. He turned his back on Katschen and began to climb down the hill. Suddenly he looked back and saw that Katschen was looking at him. The old man returned to Katschen and said, "Shu ismak?"[3] Katschen said, "Katschen." The old man said, "Ana ismi Ahmad."[4] Then the old man left with the donkey and Katschen was left alone on the hill.

◈

Suddenly it seemed to Katschen that the old man was not a real old man and the donkey was not a real donkey, but that they were more like the sights he saw at night; pictures transparent as air on the finest of all cloths. Once, the picture of a dragon appeared in Katschen's mind. If he had been able to, Katschen would have preferred to imagine a different picture, but even if the dragon had left the picture and stood in front of him, Katschen would not have been afraid. The dragon would open its mouth and spit fire, but Katschen would stand his ground and look the dragon in the face until the dragon understood that it was not a real dragon.

"The things I can touch," thought Katschen to himself, "are real," and he touched the horn on his neck. But the

1. Arabic - "Jews."
2. Arabic - "Farewell."
3. Arabic - "What is your name?"
4. Arabic - "My name is Ahmad."

horn, and his hands touching it, moved away from Katschen and he couldn't find in himself other hands with which to feel his hands. "All this is a dream," thought Katschen, and he found this to be a very strange thought. Storks flew across the sky. Katschen tried to picture in his mind the storks he could see, but the storks he imagined were not the storks he had seen, and once more Katschen did not know whether storks had flown across the sky or whether this was only a picture in a dream. And because this strange thought refused to leave him, Katschen decided to think about it until it disappeared. "I think all this is a dream, but it isn't," said Katschen to himself. "This thought," thought Katschen, "is my thought, and it's strong enough to get rid of the previous one." But as he was thinking this thought, it too moved away from him, and once again he didn't know if it was his own thought or not. "The more my thoughts roll around," thought Katschen, "the more I lose myself." And because he was looking for himself, he remembered he had once asked his mother Margarethe where was Katschen before he was born. "You are my child," said Margarethe. "When I was a little girl I went for a walk in a field of cabbages. The field was full of cabbages and in each cabbage lay a baby. All the babies were asleep and only one baby was awake. 'Do you want to be my baby?' I asked, and the baby said, 'Yes.' When I grew up I married Ernst, and we had a baby. I looked at its face and saw it was the baby I chose in the cabbage field."

Suddenly, Katschen longed to go back to the cabbage field. "I will lie inside the cabbage," he thought, "until Margarethe finds me. And when she finds me she will stay with me forever and never go up to the sky again." "The cabbage field," thought Katschen, "is near those houses with the red roofs. I'll go there and look for the cabbage field." But as he climbed down the hill he began to worry. "When I was a baby," he thought, "my body was small and it could fit inside a cabbage. Now my body is big and my legs will poke out and Margarethe will not want such a child. Now I'll have to look for the biggest cabbage in the world."

While Katschen's thoughts were revolving around the cabbage he saw a little man with curly side-locks hanging from his temples.[1] The man stood and looked at him. "This man," thought Katschen to himself, "is a sort of dwarf. The houses here are small, and the people who live in them have small bodies, and they could climb in and out of cabbages with ease." The man turned his head towards his house and called out, "A child of the Ashkenaz! A child of the Ashkenaz!"[2] Immediately, a little woman walked out of the house. The man and the woman approached Katschen and said one after the other in a strange accent:

"Where have you come from, child?"
"Who is your father?"
"Where do you live?"
"How old are you, child?"

Their words rang in Katschen's ears like some kind of music without questions or answers, played only for him to hear.

◈

"Come and eat something, child," said the little woman and took hold of Katschen's hand. When Katschen walked into the house he saw a horse and rider on the wall. For a moment

1. A Yemenite Jew. The Yemenite Jewish community immigrated to Israel en masse in 1948.
2. Ashkenazi Jews are of European origin.

it seemed to Katschen that the man on the horse was the old man he had met in the field. But the land on the wall was different, all sand dunes, and in the sky hung a crescent moon. Katschen remembered the picture in Aunt Oppenheim's room. "The rider of this horse," thought Katschen, "is the lover of the woman who lives here, and he is searching for her in the desert. And when he finds her he will get down from his horse and offer her flowers." The woman saw that Katschen was looking at the tapestry on the wall. She pointed to the horse and said in the same strange accent, "We came from there on eagles' wings."[1] A picture took shape in Katschen's mind. The man on the horse is galloping to his beloved through a cloud of sand. But as he draws near and can already see her face, a huge eagle descends from the sky, snatches the woman in its beak and carries her up and far, far away. Katschen wanted to ask the woman if the man in the picture was still riding his horse through the desert and searching for her but the woman placed a bowl of spicy-smelling food in front of him and said, "Eat, child."

Suddenly Katschen saw that on the floor, in the corner, an old man was sitting with a pipe in his mouth. A tube extended from the pipe and entered a bottle, and in the bottle there was water. Katschen, who had never seen such a strange pipe, put down his spoon and looked the old man in the face. The old man looked back at Katschen and said, "Where have you come from, child?" Katschen pondered the old man's question for a little while and said, "Cabbage." The old man fell silent and sucked at his pipe. Then he removed the end of the pipe from his mouth and asked, "Cabbage . . . kibbutz?" "Nein," said Katschen. "Cabbage

1. When the Yemenite Jews saw the planes which came to take them to Israel they believed this to be an exact fulfillment of the biblical prophecy that God would return his people "on the wings of eagles."

. . . field." The eyes of the old man widened. "A field of cabbage." The old man shook his head from right to left and from left to right and said, "Poor child. An orphan."

◈

Meanwhile the man and the woman had left and Katschen found himself alone with the old man. The old man saw that Katschen had finished his food and was sitting and looking at him, and he said, "Come here, child." Katschen went and sat down beside him. The old man thrust his hand under a nearby pillow, pulled out a book and said, "Do you know what this is, child?" Katschen looked at the book and said, "Buch."[1] The old man said, "In the tongue of the Ashkenaz it might be 'buch,' but in the holy tongue it is called 'Teyro.'"[2] Since he wanted to please the old man, Katschen repeated the word and said, "Teyro." The old man said, "And this is the Law which Moses set before the Children of Israel."[3] Katschen repeated, "And this is the Law which Moses set before the Children of Israel." The old man's face beamed. He wound the tube around the neck of the bottle and placed a sort of shawl with black stripes running across it round Katschen's neck. Once Katschen saw a man with such a shawl around his neck and asked Uncle Arthur what it was. "It's not the kind of thing," Uncle Arthur said "that people put on for decoration. These people put the shawl around their necks for their Gottesdienst."[4] Katschen thought such people were very lucky to have an enchanted shawl. They could spread the shawl in front of them and

1. German - "Book."
2. In Yemenite pronunciation - "Torah."
3. Deuteronomy 4:44.
4. German - "God worship."

see Gott through it. But when he asked Uncle Arthur what
the people saw through the shawl, Uncle Arthur said that
they saw nothing, but Gott, who sees both them and their
shawls, laughs. "There is no harm," thought Katschen to
himself, "if Gott laughs, as long as I don't upset the old
man."

The old man opened the book and read from it: "In the
beginning God created the heavens and the earth." Katschen
listened and asked, "Created?" "Created. Made," said the
old man. "The heavens and the earth?" said Katschen. "The
heavens and the earth," said the old man. Katschen said,
"And the air?" "And the air," said the old man. Katschen
said, "And the stars?" "And the stars," said the old man.
Katschen thought about what the old man had said, and
asked, "Where is God?" The old man took the end of the
pipe from the neck of the bottle and placed it inside his
mouth. For a long while he sucked at his pipe and said nothing. Bubbles rose to the surface of the water. Finally, the old
man took the pipe out of his mouth, looked at Katschen and
said, "He has neither form nor body." A picture took shape
in Katschen's mind. God makes the earth and leaves it. He
makes the sky and removes Himself to the air above the sky.
He makes the stars and removes Himself beyond them. And
after he has made the sky and the earth and the air and the
stars, there is no room left for Him in the universe, and He
gets smaller and smaller until He disappears beyond the last
star and nobody can see Him anymore. Once Margarethe
had also been in the world, but after she gave birth to
Katschen her body shrunk and removed itself from the
world, and now, when he calls out Margarethe's name, his
voice gets lost among the stars. "God," thought Katschen,
"gave birth to the world and died. And now the world asks
for God in vain. A child sees his mother for only a short

time, when he is a baby, and then, for the rest of his life, he asks for his mother who has no form and the mother who has no form asks for her child." Katschen saw that Margarethe's sorrow was no less than his own and he pictured Margarethe's own short time when she was little and lay in her cradle, and her mother, who had not yet lost her form, was still beside her.

"Mother of God," said Katschen. The old man lifted his hands into the air, a book in the one, and the end of the pipe in the other, and cried, "Be astonished O ye heavens!"[1] Then he averted his face from Katschen, closed his eyes, and only his lips moved. Suddenly Katschen saw in the face of the old man that he too had once been a baby, and was filled with wonder. The old man opened his eyes, replaced the end of the pipe on the neck of the bottle and said, "Child, He is the first and hath no beginning." Katschen remembered that he had once opened his eyes at night, in the dark, and could not see a thing and did not know where he was, and his hands groped through the air and found nothing, and at that moment he was alone in the world, and did not remember what had been and did not know what would be.

". . . the earth was without form and void," read the old man from the book, "and darkness was upon the face of the deep; and the spirit of God moved across the face of the waters. And God said: 'Let there be light.' And there was light." The wheel of the sun stood in the window and clouds sailed across. Outside a dog barked and the old man went back to blowing bubbles through the water. When Katschen looked at his face, he understood that his own sorrow, and the sorrow of the old man, and God's sorrow, were all one sorrow, and a great happiness filled his heart.

1. Jeremiah 2:12

◈

"Is this the boy?" asked the policeman who stood at the door. "This is the child," said the woman whose lover searches for her in the desert. "Come along, son," said the policeman. The old man rose from his place in the corner, lifted up his hands and cried, "The child is an orphan. He shall live with us." But the policeman placed his hand on Katschen's shoulder and led him outside. "Why did you run away from the kibbutz?" asked Herr Grossman's head which peered out of a car window. "He knows that my name is Katschen," thought Katschen. The policeman bent his knees until his head reached the same level as Katschen's and asked, "Why did you leave the kibbutz?" "I was looking for the cow," said Katschen. "You like cows?" asked the policeman, and Katschen saw in his face that he had once been a child and his mother had pressed him to her breast and he laughed, and she said, "Again?" and he laughed and said, "Again."

At the gate of the kibbutz Herr Grossman got out of the car and said to Katschen, "Come along, let's go." A picture formed in Katschen's mind. Herr Grossman returns to the kibbutz and says the name "Katschen." A man in blue waves a knife and says, "What did he say? What did he say?" A woman descends from a ladder, her saw cutting through the air, and says, "He said it! He said it!" Katschen looked into the policeman's face and said, "The cow is not in the kibbutz." The policeman laughed and said, "Maybe she went to the fields to look for a boy." Herr Grossman said, "He's been placed in our care." The policeman said, "We'll see," and they drove away.

On the way, the policeman pulled the steering wheel right and left and left and right and sang, "Ti-na Ti-na,

come to Palesti-na." Katschen thought of Tina, sailing
across the sea past the strip of gold which was Zypern, with
the prow of her ship turned towards Palestina. Birds rose
from the fields. "And who do *you* love?" asked the policeman. "It's because he's thinking of Tina that he thinks of
other people's loves," thought Katschen, and said, "Avigail."
But when he tried to think about Avigail she faded into the
distance and he could not remember where she was or what
she looked like.

◇

When they reached the police station the policeman
said, "Sit down," and went away. "All I ever do," thought
Katschen to himself, "is come and go, and come and go."
But as he was mulling this over he was uncertain again
whether it was he who came and went, or other people came
and went while he stayed in the same place.

Next to Katschen sat a woman. Perfume rose from her
body. "Between your legs," said the woman, "lives a little
dwarf and he does what he likes." This amazed Katschen and
he asked, "What does he do?" The woman said, "At night,
he wakes up, stands up straight, and goes off to look for another house." "And does he find it?" asked Katschen. The
woman smoothed her fingers between her legs, rubbed her
shoulder against Katschen's shoulder and, in a voice whose
melody unfurled (like a roll of silk), said, "Come to me my
prince. Come to me my dove. What you lack you can always
get from me." Katschen looked into the woman's face and
saw that her lips were red, and her hair was gold and she had
gold rings on her fingers, and thought to himself that the
dwarf could hear this melody and was pricking up his ears,
longing for her, and going out to look for her. "When you

grow up your dwarf will come to me as well," said the woman, and Katschen was filled with joy. Then the policeman walked in and said, "Come on," and Katschen followed him.

◇

In a room with green walls policemen were sitting and eating. Through a hatch in the wall Katschen saw a huge pot and a fat cook with a white hat on his head. When the cook saw Katschen he looked up at the ceiling and barked like a dog. Then he stuck his head into the hatch and asked, "Do you want a cat as well?" "Ja," said Katschen, and the cook meowed like a cat. Katschen remembered the song Aunt Oppenheim used to sing him until he fell asleep—"Ein Hund kahm in die Küche":

> A dog came to the kitchen
> And stole the cook's fresh stew
> The cook picked up the carving knife
> And cut the dog in two
> All the other dogs came round
> And wondered what to do
> They wrote these words above the grave
> For everyone to view:
> A dog came to the kitchen
> And stole the cook's fresh stew
> The cook picked up the carving knife
> And cut the dog in two
> All the other dogs came round
> And wondered what to do
> They wrote these words above the grave

For everyone to view:
A dog came to the kitchen
And stole the cook's fresh stew

"This story has no end," thought Katschen, and decided to go back to the beginning. But when he went back to the beginning it seemed to him that even the first dog who came to the kitchen was not a real dog, but was only the story of the dog which the other dogs had written on the gravestone. "This story doesn't have a beginning either," thought Katschen, and was filled with wonder.

"Eat!" said the policeman. Katschen dipped his spoon into the bowl and took a sip of the soup. When the taste of the soup entered his mouth, doubt left his mind. "The soup I am eating is the soup I took from the cook," thought Katschen, and understood that the story begins with the taste of the stew.

◇

That night Katschen slept in the policeman's house. There was another man there, whose name was Naim, and the two of them rolled a dice across a wooden board divided into lots of triangles. The policeman sang "Tina Tina come to Palestina" and from time to time asked Katschen if he fancied some tea. When Naim's eyes met Katschen's eyes, Naim said, "So how are you doing?" and Katschen said, "Fine."
In the morning, the policeman hit an egg until its shell broke open, and then poured it into a frying pan. When the edges of the egg turned brown, the policeman tilted the frying pan and the egg slid onto a plate. He placed the plate before Katschen and said, "Eat!" Then the policeman brought

Katschen to a man at the police station and went away.
Katschen looked at the man's face and saw that he was thinking hard. "Right" said the man, "let's play a little game. I'll
say a word, and you immediately say what comes into your
head. 'Old.'" For a moment it seemed to Katschen that the
man was calling him "old" and he was surprised. But when
he thought about it he understood that the word had only
been said so that he could hear it and immediately say what
came into his head. Katschen remembered Uncle Arthur's
cane and said "Bird." The man wrote down what Katschen
had said and said "Family." Katschen said "Cow" and
the man said "Milk." Katschen said "Arab" and the man
said "War." Katschen said "Kibbutz" and the man said
"Mother." Katschen said "Zypern" and the man said "Sea."
Katschen said "Avigail" and the man said "Bible." Katschen
said "Pipe" and the man said "Father." Katschen said "Herr
Druck" and the man said "Who's that?" Katschen turned
over the question in his mind and finally said "Schakal."[1]
The man looked at his notes for a long time. Then he raised
his head and said, "So, you think people are like animals?"
"Not all of them," said Katschen and the man frowned.
"Now draw something," he said. Katschen picked up a pencil and drew a dragon. "Right" said the man, "and who is
the man you drew?" "That's a strange question," thought
Katschen. Had the man asked, "What did you draw?" he
would have answered, "A dragon." And had he asked, "Is
this a man?" he would have answered, "It's a dragon." But
since he wanted the man to be satisfied, Katschen drew Herr
Druck with a hat on his head next to the dragon. The man
looked at Herr Druck and asked, "So who is that?" Katschen

1. German - jackal

said, "Herr Druck." "Herr Druck . . . who is he?" asked
the man, and Katschen said, "Schakal." The man frowned
for the second time and said, "Now tell me what you dream
about." Katschen remembered and said, "Mad Sarah." The
man's face lit up and he wrote something down. Then he
said, "And who is this Sarah?" and Katschen said he didn't
know. The man frowned for the third time. "So," he said,
"now go outside and play." But Katschen remembered that
the hall outside was empty and he did not know who he
could play with. "Another game," said Katschen. The man
eased himself back in his chair and said, "Good. We'll play
with words again." "Now," said Katschen, "I am first. Photosynthesis." The man looked at Katschen and his eyes
widened. His lips moved but no words came out. "He only
knows how to play," thought Katschen to himself, "when he
goes first."

◇

The policeman came back. He placed his hand on Katschen's
shoulder and said, "Your uncle is no longer with us." "If Uncle Arthur is no longer with us," thought Katschen to himself, "he must be with someone else." "And your aunt," continued the policeman, "has returned to Vienna." "Now,"
thought Katschen, "Aunt Oppenheim will meet her lover
and he will offer her flowers." Then the policeman turned to
the man and said, "His father is alive but he . . ." and the
policeman leaned over the man and whispered something
into his ear. The man said, "The boy is also . . . ," and
whispered something into the policeman's ear. Katschen
looked at the policeman and said, "I'll be with Ernst." The

man said, "No. He has to go to . . . ," and whispered something into the policeman's ear. The policeman looked at the man, then looked at Katschen and said, "We'll see." Outside, the policeman raised his eyes to the sky and sighed. Then he bent his knees until his head was at the same level as Katschen's and said, "Your father is ill. Do you know?" and Katschen said "Ja." The policeman sighed again and said, "That man doesn't want you to go to your father." Katschen told the policeman that the man makes up games but doesn't know how to play them. The policeman laughed and said, "You know what, I'll take you to your father."

On the way, Katschen told the policeman a woman in the police station told him that the dwarf between his legs would come to her one day. The policeman laughed and said, "That was Shifra. Your dwarf would do better to go to Avigail." Katschen was filled with affection for the policeman and thought to himself, "I hope Tina comes to Palestina." Then the policeman led Katschen to a man selling ice cream and the man handed Katschen a green ice cream studded with nuts. And when Katschen passed his tongue over the ice cream he remembered the ice cream Uncle Arthur had bought him once, and understood that Uncle Arthur was dead.

◈

"Ah," said a man dressed in white coat, "Ernst is the man you're looking for. He's quiet. You can see him." When the man left to look for Ernst, a woman sidled up to the policeman and said, "The clothes on your body are very nice." The policeman laughed and said, "the clothes on your body are very nice too." The woman said, "You're thinking about something else." The policeman asked, "What am I thinking about?" The woman said, "What I'm thinking about." The policeman looked at Katschen's face and said, "You see? There's no difference between the people here and the people outside." Suddenly Katschen felt afraid that the Ernst who was here would not be his father. Meanwhile, the man in the white coat had returned with another man and said, "This is Ernst." Ernst pointed at the policeman and said in German, "He is not my son." "No," said the man in the white coat and pointed at Katschen. "This is your son. The policeman just came with him." Ernst snatched a quick glance at Katschen's face and immediately turned back to the policeman. "Now," he said, "I have to talk with my son about my will." The man in white hesitated for a moment and then said, "All right. Go with him to your room." Ernst turned his back and walked away, and Katschen walked behind him.

In the room, Ernst stood by the window and looked outside and Katschen knew from his back that he was his father. "Verstehst du mich?"[1] said Ernst, and Katschen, who did not know what he had to understand, said "Ja." Ernst spoke with his back to Katschen. "You must choose. Small and important or big and worthless?" At that moment Katschen knew with absolute clarity that if he made the wrong choice he would lose his father again. The sound of a bell rose from the street and a man shouted, "Paraffin! Paraffin!" "Big and worthless," said Katschen. "Gutt!" said Ernst and opened the window. "Outside!" First he held Katschen by the waist and lowered him through the window until Katschen's feet touched the ground. Then he too climbed out through the window. When they stood outside Ernst said, "One and one are one," and the two of them left.

1. German - "Do you understand me?"

◇

When they reached the fields on the outskirts of the town Ernst looked over Katschen's head and said in German, "Now we will rise to the heavens in a chariot of fire." Then he placed himself in the middle of the road and spread out his arms. A truck the size of a mountain screeched to a halt and almost touched Ernst's body. Out of the window glared a head with a black beard and shouted, "Are you mad?" Ernst lifted his eyes to the man and said, "Elijah." The man opened his mouth and his eyes widened. "You know who I am?" he asked, and Ernst said, "Yes." Ernst climbed up and seated himself next to the man with the beard and Katschen climbed up after him. The man closed the door and they drove off. The noise was deafening. "Who are you?" shouted the man, but Ernst closed his eyes and said nothing. The man looked at Katschen and shouted, "Where does he know me from?" and Katschen, who did not know what to say, said, "Maybe from Jerusalem." "From Jerusalem?" shouted the man, and Katschen shouted, "Yes." The man fell silent, immersed in thought. Then he looked at Katschen again and shouted, "The British Army?" and Katschen, who did not know what the question meant, shouted, "Yes." "Ah," shouted the man, "I know." When the fields came to an end they went through hills, and when they came out of the hills another town stretched before them. The truck stopped in the middle of the town and the man with the beard slapped Ernst across the shoulder and said, "Wake up, mate. Here we are." Ernst also said, "Here we are." Then he opened his eyes and climbed down to the pavement without looking at the man. "What's the matter with him?" said the man to Katschen, and Katschen said, "He's thinking." "Oh well," said the man, and gave Katschen his hand. "If you ever need anything you can always rely on Elijah Zisskind. Those were good times in the British Army." Ernst had already disappeared around the corner of the street and Katschen ran after him, shouting "Vater, Vater." Ernst did not stop, but slowed his pace. After they had walked together some way through the streets of the town, Katschen asked, "Vater, wohin gehst du?"[1] Ernst stopped. He looked at Katschen and said, "Never ask a question like that again." "Warum?"[2] asked Katschen. "Because time," said Ernst, "is not a line, and place is not a space." And although Katschen did not know what his father was saying, he understood that from now on both of them would look only through the eye in their foreheads.

◈

Meanwhile the day had grown dark. Katschen saw Ernst's shadow on the pavement and said, "Schatten."[3] Ernst stretched out his hands in front of him, distorting his fingers into talons, and said, "Ratten."[4] Katschen looked at Ernst's hands and said, "Jesus Christus." Ernst laughed and said, "Ich."[5] Katschen laughed too and said, "Auch ich."[6] Smells of cooking wafted out of the houses. Suddenly Katschen longed to know whether his father remembered he had once sat in the armchair with slippers on his feet and Katschen had scattered the silverware around him. "Ja," said Ernst, and Katschen was not at all surprised that his father had answered the question before he heard it. But then Ernst

1. German - "Father, where are you going?"
2. German - "Why?"
3. German - "Shadow."
4. German - "Rats."
5. German - "Me"; also Hebrew - "A man."
6. German - "Me too."

saw something that frightened him, and said, "Nein," and
Katschen understood that his father remembered the sights
but hadn't the strength to look at them.

Since Katschen was thinking of memories, he remembered Frau Kurtz's photograph album. It was because of
Yoachim that the paths of Frau Kurtz and Aunt Oppenheim
crossed for a time in Vienna. And when they both found
their way to Palestine they made it a rule to see each other,
one week at Aunt Oppenheim's house and the following
week at Frau Kurtz's house. When Frau Kurtz saw Katschen
with Aunt Oppenheim, she always said, "Look, look, we
have a special guest today," and Katschen knew that Frau
Kurtz would then say "And it just so happens that I have
sweet biscuits." Frau Kurtz would take down a tin box, upon
which brown cows grazed in a field of flowers, and extract
from it two sugar-coated biscuits. Frau Kurtz put the
biscuits onto a plate and the plate in front of Katschen.
Katschen was convinced that the two biscuits were for the
two times that Frau Kurtz had said "Look" and hoped that
one day Frau Kurtz would break her habit and say, "Look,
look, look" and place three biscuits before him. Aunt Oppenheim and Frau Kurtz sipped coffee with cream from
china cups and Katschen drank cocoa. Then Frau Kurtz
picked up the photograph album and opened it where
Yoachim lay. First, they looked at the photograph of
Yoachim as he was when he still had both his legs. Then they
looked at Yoachim as he was when he had only one of his own
legs, and the other, which was made of wood, was stuck to
his body, and said, "Der arme Kerl."[1] And when Katschen
asked if they had chopped down a tree to make Yoachim's
wooden leg, Frau Kurtz said that that was not the point. The

---

1. German - "The poor fellow."

point was that Yoachim had given his leg to Germany, and Germany gave him beautiful decorations to pin to his chest. A picture formed in Katschen's mind. Yoachim enters a shop and looks at the decorations displayed there. He points his finger and says, "That one and that one." The German takes down the decorations which Yoachim pointed out and places them in front of him. Yoachim lifts his leg and places it on the counter next to the decorations. The German picks up a saw and cuts off Yoachim's leg. Yoachim pins the decorations to his chest and hops out of the shop on one leg.

In Frau Kurtz's photograph album there were other people as well. Some stood alone and some in groups, and at the end of the album, where it was written "Palestina," the people had taken off their elegant clothes and stood in short trousers. Behind their backs were mountains strewn with boulders and between the boulders grew thorn bushes. Frau Kurtz placed a finger over the face of one man and said, "Der ist schon tot."[1] But when she removed her finger and his face reappeared, the dead man smiled, and did not leave his place.

◈

"Before my eyes," said Ernst suddenly, "there is glass and a bird pecking at it all the time." Katschen looked at his father's face and saw that his eyes did not see what was in front of him. "Before my eyes," said Ernst again, "there is glass and a bird pecking at it all the time." A picture took shape in Katschen's mind. The bird approaches the glass, its eyes getting bigger and bigger. Then he heard the sound of the beak pecking at the glass. The sight and the sound emerged in

---

1. German - "That one's dead already."

German and Katschen was filled with wonder that even a picture needed a language to draw itself. If Ernst had spoken Hebrew, thought Katschen, he would have looked through the glass without seeing it and the bird would have flown elsewhere. "Vater," said Katschen, "Warum sprichst du nicht Ivrit?"[1] "Hebrew?" said Ernst, and the very word sounded like German in his mouth. "Ja," said Katschen, "Hebrew." Ernst was silent for a long while, and then he said in a strange melody, "Be-reyshis boro elohim es ha-shamayim ve-es ho-oretz."[2] Suddenly, Katschen was filled with fear that his father would leave him and said, "Before my eyes, too, there is glass and a bird pecking at it." "The same glass," said Ernst, and Katschen understood that his father was not mad. "And the bird?" asked Katschen. "And the bird," said Ernst. A distant memory came back to Katschen's mind. Margarethe is asleep in her bed, her face to the wall. His father lifts him out of the cradle and brings him ever so slowly towards his face. And through the lenses of Ernst's glasses Katschen sees the eyes of his father coming closer and closer.

◇

Ernst went through the door of an inn and Katschen followed him in. Once they were inside Katschen saw that the innkeeper's head was big, and his body carried his head as though it had done it a favor by transporting it a short distance and now that it had been delivered as promised, the head refused to get off and wobbled on the thin neck. "Ein Bett,"[3] said Ernst, and Katschen knew his father could see what he saw, and was not asking for a bed for himself but for

---

1. German - "Father, why don't you speak Hebrew?"
2. Hebrew - "In the beginning God created the heavens and the earth."
3. German - "A bed."

the innkeeper to rest his head. "Für zwei?"[1] asked the innkeeper. Ernst looked at the innkeeper's head and said, "Farzweifelt."[2] The innkeeper took a bunch of keys and opened the door for them. In the room stood a large wooden bed, with legs carved into the shape of lions' feet. Ernst looked at the legs of the bed and said, "Ein Löwe."[3] The innkeeper's head nodded violently. "Zehr angenehm. Friedman,"[4] he said, and walked off. Ernst knelt down and touched the lion's feet. "Schau,"[5] he said, "ein Löwe." "Vater," said Katschen, "hast du geld bei dir?"[6] But Ernst only smiled to himself and said again, "Ein Löwenbett."[7] Suddenly, his father took on the shape of a lion in Katschen's mind. "Soon," thought Katschen, "the lion will get onto his couch and fall into a lion's sleep." And instead of being filled with wonder that his father had turned into a lion, Katschen turned himself into a lion cub. For a long while the lions paced around the room. Manes covered their necks and the movement of their feet was slow and serene. From time to time the big lion growled and the little lion answered with a growl. Afterwards, the two lions climbed into bed and stared at the ceiling of the room with yellow eyes divided by a black streak.

◈

In the morning, Ernst looked into the mirror and said, "Gott, wie hässlich dieser Kopf ist."[8] Ernst looked at his face

1. German - "For two?"
2. Yiddish - "Full of sorrow."
3. German - "A lion."
4. Yiddish - "Pleased to meet you. (My name is) Friedman."
5. German - "Look."
6. German - "Father, have you any money with you?"
7. German - "A lionbed."
8. German - "God, how ugly this face is."

as though he had never seen it before in his life and was re-
lieved that the face looking back at him was not his. Once,
Katschen looked at Uncle Arthur looking at his face in the
mirror and saw a sadness in Uncle Arthur's eyes that the
face trailed around with him all his life. But Frau Kurtz
looked in the mirror as though it never crossed her mind
that the face looking back at her was not her own. On the
piano in her house stood the head of Beethoven, and Frau
Kurtz looked at this face too without amazement, as though
it was the only face he had. Once Frau Kurtz had taken
Katschen with her to the market and by the way she was
walking Katschen saw that she was sure what happened to
her was bound to happen and that what didn't happen was
bound not to happen. This aroused a kind of anger in
Katschen and he distorted his face like a madman. The people who happened to pass them looked at Katschen in surprise, and Frau Kurtz, who noticed the looks on their faces,
looked down at Katschen. But Katschen quickly put on a
different face, as though he too was sure everything was as
it should be, and Frau Kurtz, who could not understand
what had suddenly gone wrong, was overcome with embar-
rassment. In the market, Frau Kurtz bought a chicken.
When she returned home she chopped off the chicken's
head. Then she poured out its entrails and cut off its wings.
And when the chicken was left without a head, and without
entrails, and without wings, Frau Kurtz cut off its legs.
Katschen wasn't at all sorry about what happened to the
chicken, but Frau Kurtz's eye took on a look of satisfaction,
as though she was sure the deeds she was doing were her
own deeds, and it was only proper they be done just as she
was doing them. At the table, Katschen tasted the dish and
praised Frau Kurtz on the taste of "the dead bird," but Frau

Kurtz was not dismayed and merely commented that in German, one says Huhn.[1]

◈

The innkeeper's head was in the kitchen. "A fried egg?" he asked, and Ernst extended his arm, pointed at his head, and said in German, "This head is holy." Katschen said, "Yes," and the innkeeper put two fried eggs in front of them. Ernst looked down at the fried egg and said, "What does this eye see?" and Katschen said, "Iss, Vater."[2] Ernst put the fried egg into his mouth and swallowed it in one go. Then he turned to an invisible audience and said, "Never laugh at a big head." It seemed then to Katschen that his father was a kind of prophet, who knows what was, and knows what will be, but Katschen did not know if his father knew what is. "Herr Löwe," said the innkeeper in a strange sort of German, "will you be staying tonight as well?" "Herr Friedman," said Ernst, "when a man comes into the world he stays until he leaves." Katschen heard this and was filled with joy that his father remembered the innkeeper's name, but Ernst, as though he saw what Katschen had thought, said, "God did not make a man without a name. He made Friedman." "May God bless you and everything you do," said the innkeeper. Ernst thrust his hand into his trouser pocket, pulled out a leather wallet, and placed it before Katschen. Katschen drew two notes from the wallet and placed them in the innkeeper's hand. The innkeeper put the two notes into his pocket and said, "When my wife, may she

1. German - hen.
2. German - "Eat, Father."

rest in peace, was still alive, everything was better." "Him too," said Ernst, and pointed to Katschen. "His wife is dead." The innkeeper's eyes widened and he looked at Katschen. Then he moved his eyes back to Ernst and saw what he saw.

◈

When they walked out of the inn, rain was falling on the town. Katschen looked at the rain and said, "It's raining." Ernst too looked at the rain and asked, "What's raining?" At first it seemed to Katschen there was no sense to this question but when he turned it over in his mind he understood that it had only come out of what he himself had said. When Katschen was small it had rained, and Uncle Arthur had taken off his coat and wrapped Katschen in it so that the rain would not wet him, and the coat was filled with the smell of Uncle Arthur. "Vater," said Katschen, "Onkel Arthur ist gestorben."[1] Ernst turned his head towards Katschen and looked at his mouth. "If Ernst understood that his brother is dead," thought Katschen to himself, "he would look into my eyes." Then Ernst looked away and walked on, and from the sight of his back Katschen understood that he was pacing out "Arthur ist gestorben": an "Arthur" pace, an "ist" pace, and a "gestorben" pace, and again "Arthur," and "ist" and "gestorben," and again and again. Water dripped from Ernst's ears. Suddenly, Katschen longed to tell his father that Uncle Arthur always said "mein kind," but since he knew Ernst was thinking that Arthur died because his father was born, he said nothing. Katschen had once seen a picture of his grandfather. The photograph was yellow and out of the

---

1. German - "Uncle Arthur is dead."

brown suit peeped a round watch. "Your grandfather," said Uncle Arthur, "the father of Ernst and myself, rode a horse in the army of Franz-Joseph." A beard sprouted from both sides of his chin, and under his nose was a thick moustache whose ends twirled upwards. But by then, the grandfather who looked out of the photograph was already "gestorben," and when Katschen asked, Uncle Arthur told him that the horse his grandfather rode was also "gestorben." The grandfather's eyes looked through Katschen to some other place, and Katschen, who saw what he saw, decided that when he was big, he would find a picture of the horse and place it in front of the picture of his grandfather.

◇

Suddenly, Ernst said, "Margarethe liebt den Arthur,"[1] and Katschen remembered that Uncle Arthur told him Margarethe had chosen Ernst because he was the more stubborn, but Ernst, who was afraid to lose her, had lost his mind. Then Ernst turned his head towards Katschen and looked at him as though he had never seen him. "Und wo ist Margarethe?"[2] he asked, and Katschen said, "Im Himmel."[3]

When Margarethe was already dead, snow covered the town and Uncle Arthur took Katschen out to see the snow, and when Katschen stepped in the snow he remembered the sweetness of porridge he had eaten when he was a baby. On that day it seemed to Katschen that if the whole world turned white Margarethe would come back to him. But some of the branches on the trees remained grey, and by evening

1. German - "Margarethe the beloved of Arthur."
2. German - "And where is Margarethe?"
3. German - "In the sky."

the snow was already mixed with mud. "Und wo bin ich?"[1] asked Ernst, and Katschen, who did not know how to answer his father, was silent. A woman dressed in black walked out of a gate in the wall. Katschen understood that Margarethe was already a long way from Ernst and that his father sees what he sees and his heart is broken. And since he wished to make Ernst forget his sorrow, he told him that one day the dwarf between his legs would come to a woman he had met at the police station.

◆

Meanwhile, Katschen and his father had entered the alley-ways of the market. "Now," thought Katschen, "I will raise my hand and everything will freeze." Katschen raised his hand but nothing changed. A vendor weighed tomatoes and a woman felt pears. Katschen remembered Aunt Oppenheim's foot that was white, with the little toe bent upwards, and covered with a thick crust. "Vater," he said, "Der Fuss von Tante Oppenheim."[2] "Ja," said Ernst, "Eine traurige Geschichte."[3] From his father's words Katschen understood that raising his hand had been act of foolishness, and he raised his hand again to make everything stay as it was. Katschen's hand made the woman put tomatoes in a basket and the vendor stretch out his arm to pick up an apple. "Und alles ist eine Geige,"[4] said Ernst suddenly. "Alles ist eine Geige," repeated Katschen after Ernst. "Und alles ist eine Geige," said Ernst for the second time. "What my father says," thought Katschen, "is not exactly the same as I said."

1. German - "And where am I?"
2. German - "Aunt Oppenheim's foot."
3. German - "A sad affair."
4. German - "And all is a violin."

And in order to remove the doubt, Katschen again said, "Alles ist eine geige." "Und alles ist eine geige," said Ernst for the third time. Katschen looked around and saw that "Alles ist eine geige," was sheer nonsense, while "Und alles ist eine geige" was the naked truth. "My father hears smells," thought Katschen to himself, and he too said, "Und alles ist eine geige."

◈

Katschen and his father had by now left the town and were walking through the fields. Where the fields ended stood a mountain, its peak wrapped in clouds like a white bandage. Suddenly, Katschen understood that what was had already been, and what was to be would not be. "Vater," said Katschen, "ein Berg."[1] Ernst lifted his eyes to the mountain and said softly "Ja." Katschen saw there were brown spots on the back of Ernst's hand and touched them. Ernst took Katschen's hand and brought it to his stomach. At that moment Katschen knew that the difference between himself and his father was getting smaller and smaller and that all that would remain of it would be the size of their bodies. Birds passed over their heads. Ernst looked at the birds until they disappeared behind the mountain. Then he looked at Katschen. And when Katschen looked into Ernst's eyes his soul turned over. "My father's eyes can see!" thought Katschen. He knew that a great disaster was at hand but his heart quivered with happiness. "Weist du wer ich bin?"[2] Katschen asked his father. "Ja," said Ernst, "Katschen."

1. German - "A mountain."
2. German - "Do you know who I am?"